THE PEOPLE vs. LARRY FLYNT

THE PEOPLE vs. LARRY FLYNT

SCREENPLAY AND NOTES BY

Scott Alexander & Larry Karaszewski

AFTERWORD WITH

Milos Forman

A Newmarket Shooting Script™ Series Book

NEWMARKET PRESS • NEW YORK

For our wives, who put up with Hustler *talk for three years.*
And for our agent, who did what he said he would do.

First Edition
96 97 98 99   10 9 8 7 6 5 4 3 2 1

Library of Congress Cataloging-in-Publication Data

Alexander, Scott (Scott M.)
    The people vs. Larry Flynt : the shooting script : screenplay by Scott Alexander & Larry Karaszewski;
introduction by Milos Forman. p. cm. — (A Newmarket shooting script series book) ISBN 1-55704-305-1
(paperback); 1-55704-313-2 (hardcover).   1. Flynt, Larry—Drama. I. Karaszewski, Larry. II. People vs.
Larry Flynt (Motion picture). III. Title. IV. Series. PN1997.P4565 1996 791.43'72—dc20   96-31471 CIP

Quantity Purchases

Companies, professional groups, clubs, and other organizations may qualify for special terms when ordering
quantities of this title. For information, write Special Sales, Newmarket Press,
18 East 48th Street, New York, New York 10017, call (212) 832-3575, or fax (212) 832-3629.

Book design by Tania Garcia

Manufactured in the United States of America.

CONTENTS

Columbia Pictures presents, in association with Phoenix Pictures, an Ixtlan Production of A Milos Forman Film *The People vs. Larry Flynt*. Directed by Milos Forman and written by Scott Alexander & Larry Karaszewski, the film stars Woody Harrelson, Courtney Love, and Edward Norton. Brett Harrelson, Vincent Schiavelli, Crispin Glover, James Cromwell, and Miles Chapin also star. The film features appearances by political consultant James Carville, *Good Day New York* correspondent Donna Hanover, and New York University Professor of Law Burt Neuborne. Oliver Stone, Janet Yang, and Michael Hausman are the producers. Philippe Rousselot, A.F.C., is the director of photography, Patrizia Von Brandenstein is the production designer, with Theodor Pistek and Arianne Phillips designing the costumes. The film was edited by Christopher Tellefsen.

INTRODUCTION

BY SCOTT ALEXANDER & LARRY KARASZEWSKI

"Who are they makin' a movie about?!"

"Larry Flynt?! That guy's disgusting!!"

"Typical Hollywood, with its perverted ideas of entertainment! Who are the sleazebags who thought of this?!"

Well ... we are. Blame us. Two regular Joes with wives and kids. We thought it was an amazing tale: the crudest, lewdest publisher of porn ever seen, a man most noted for his shameless vulgarity ... achieving significance in a major First Amendment victory.

We've always been attracted to eccentrics. We started our career writing *Problem Child,* one of the stranger hybrids on record. Unfortunately, our dreams of dark adult subversion got retooled into crummy kiddie slapstick, and we quickly found ourselves typecast: the guys who write family films about serial killers, sterility, and kidnapping.

This led to unemployment.

So, frustrated and wanting to reinvigorate our lives, we wrote a script, on spec, just to please ourselves. This was *Ed Wood.*

It was untraditional: a biography of someone who didn't deserve a biography. A Z-grade hack notable for his failures. But we identified with his passion. Our challenge was to take an Anti-Great Man, someone who screwed up everything and angered everyone around him ... and create empathy. Get an audience to root for his upside-down goals. Once finished, we gave the script to the one filmmaker in the world who we thought could get it made: Tim Burton. He was so taken with it that he shot our first draft. The movie achieved international acclaim, won two Oscars, and rescued us from the dungheap.

But Hollywood pigeonholes you quickly. Now we had a new reputation: the guys who write biopics of weirdos. Being enterprising types, we recognized a short-lived window of opportunity—we could come in with the freakiest, most inexplicable idea imaginable, and somebody would probably pay us to write it. So we proposed *Larry Flynt*.

We had followed Flynt's life for many years. In 1983, when we were college roommates, he hijacked the front page of the *L.A. Times*. Every day, there was a newer, stranger story: He's running for President... he's got stolen FBI surveillance tapes... he's suing Caspar Weinberger... he's wearing a diaper in a courtroom. We laughed our heads off. Larry was one of the primo American lunatics.

Ten years later, we remembered him. It was an extraordinary life—born in a log cabin, self-made multimillionaire, created an absurdly explicit porn magazine, married a stripper who later died of AIDS, became born again, was shot and paralyzed at a courthouse—powerful, fascinating material. It was astonishing that one man had done all this. Yet people were so repulsed by Larry that he had never been documented. There was no biography. It was a great untold story.

And to us, he also made a perfect movie protagonist—because Larry's so darn pushy. Development execs often complain that a script's hero is too "reactive." Well, that's not Larry's problem. He chased trouble, often trying to get arrested to make his point. Also, like Ross Perot years later, he threw millions behind publicizing his self-obsessed political vision. He pioneered TV-age media manipulation. Occasionally, somebody asked us why we weren't writing the Hugh Hefner, or Bob Guccione story. Those guys are bigger, richer, more successful.

Yes—but they're also complacent. Larry took his ill-gotten wealth and used it to create anarchy.

In Hollywood, when you want to get paid to write a script, you verbally "pitch" it. Like actors, we worked out a forty-five-minute presentation. But it needed a dress rehearsal, a run-through to see how it played. So we set up a meeting with Columbia Pictures, the studio that had abandoned *Ed Wood*. We figured if they wouldn't make that movie, they sure as hell wouldn't make this one! But we could use them as a sounding board.

Simultaneously, we sent an outline to Oliver Stone (see page 185). We didn't know him, but he seemed a natural fit for the material: controversy, America, lawsuits, wheelchairs. We crossed our fingers, hoping he'd respond....

The next day, we went into Columbia—and the meeting took an unexpected detour: They loved it. They understood it. The executives were giddily jumping up and down—"It's a Capra movie with porn! Don't take it anywhere else, we're buyin' it!" Then Oliver expressed interest, and so we all teamed up.

The studio commenced us: Go write it!

First we did our research, which took about four months. At this stage, the project was an unauthorized biography, so we didn't have access to Flynt's materials. Fortunately, we had a mole in his organization, who stole us a copy of every issue of *Hustler,* going back twenty years. These were invaluable (for the articles, naturally). *Hustler* is a completely self-obsessed publication—semioticians would call it "solipsistic." So there were endless stories about Larry, Larry's opinions, Larry's antics, and Larry's magazine itself.

We also ran a fifteen-year database search in the *New York Times, L.A. Times, Washington Post, Time,* and *Newsweek.* This generated thousands of pages— Larry has such a public life, every time he burps he holds a press conference. We tracked down court transcripts, trying to use Larry's own words whenever possible. Most interestingly, many shadowy ex-associates of Larry started contacting us: "Hi, I was Larry's cook." "Hi, I edited the magazine till Larry screwed me over." "Hi, I'm Larry's forgotten child." "Hi, I'm Timothy Leary—Larry was my best friend." We took all these people out to lunch, and they regaled us with stories. They also supplied us with yet more articles about Larry. The only people we drew a line at were those who demanded money for information: one, because it seemed unethical; and two, because we're too cheap.

After crunching this mountain of material, we ended up with two gigantic notebooks. They were organized by periods in Larry's life: early Ohio, born-again Christian, DeLorean trial, etc. Then we took hundreds of interesting quotations from Larry and arranged them by category: Larry on politics. Larry on censorship. Larry on *Hustler...* many of these got worked into our dialogue.

Next, we had to figure out tone. As a rule, we write movies about dark, disturbing subjects, onto which we impose a sunny, cheerful attitude. The result is fraught with tension, but hopefully palatable. Dramatizing Larry Flynt was walking a tightrope—include too many contemptible events, and the audience turns off. Include too many self-important events, and the movie becomes a whitewash. We weren't out to glorify him—we just wanted to tell his story.

There were numerous tonal pitfalls to avoid: Too sleazy. Too campy. Too preachy. The milieu is pornography . . . but we were writing an R-rated major studio feature, not an X-rated stag film. So we diffused the raunchiness in a few ways. One, porno is presented as almost silly, so ridiculous it's not worth getting upset over. And two, the nastiest images and ideas are always played off-screen while we focus on people's comic reactions.

But in constructing our script, the most important element was . . . the structure. We believe that the secret to a biopic is knowing where the three acts are in someone's life. Most biographies seem compelled to follow the subject from cradle to grave. The result ends up cramming in too much, skimming the surface, and being uninvolving. So we only focus on the years that matter: *Ed Wood* had five. Larry Flynt had about fifteen.

Then the film got structured around its theme: A poor country boy believes in the possibility of America. In the land of freedom, he's able to make tons of money off porn. But then he gets shot, and the country is glad. There's no investigation. Larry is shocked, then outraged that his America doesn't care. So he loses faith . . . and commits his fortune to destroying the country. He creates mayhem. But then he finds himself in a scandalous lawsuit with a highly respected man. It gets to the Supreme Court, and surprisingly, they side with Larry. The country and the man have come around. Larry can believe in America again.

The three acts seemed clear: A prologue with Larry as a little boy. Page ten—he starts *Hustler.* End of act one—his success gets him arrested. Act two—he becomes politicized. Middle of act two—he gets shot. Rest of act two—he takes revenge on America. End of act two—he gets locked up in a mental asylum. Act three—the Falwell case. Larry regains meaning in his life, and ends in a victory at the Supreme Court.

This story arc dovetailed nicely with the changing eras. The first half is the '70s—hedonism, sexual revolution, radical politics, anything goes. Then Larry gets shot and disappears for five years. When he returns, it's the '80s—and things are different. Reagan is President, and the country has become conservative. The daring raunchiness of *Hustler* seems passé and inappropriate. So Larry shifts his attentions to bigger agendas....

Ending at the Supreme Court also fulfilled our cardinal Anti-Biopic rule: Know when to get out. When you have a subversive hero, you need to justify the time the audience spends with him. We address this by giving our screwballs an ending that gives purpose to their lives, closure to the movie, and uplift to the audience. Ed Wood unknowingly made the worst film of all time, but in closing, he knows he'll be remembered. Larry Flynt is indisputably a man of smut, but at the Supreme Court, he becomes a man of history. He might have set out just wanting to make a buck...but by the end, Larry forced an important decision that protects all speech.

If the movie's plot motor was the fight for free speech, then Larry's relationship with Althea became its heart. Larry had thousands of sex partners, but Althea was the love of his life. They were two people put on Earth to be with each other—strong-willed, explosive, and deviant. She also tied into our structured story: They meet before he starts the magazine. She grows with him, forcing her opinions into *Hustler.* But after his shooting, the steady availability of drugs entraps her, and she becomes a junkie. Eventually she contracts AIDS. After she dies, we did a bit of dramatic legerdemain and found a quote from Jerry Falwell: "AIDS is a plague. These perverted lifestyles have to stop...." In our script, this confluence of events is the catalyst for Larry regaining his passion, then climactically taking Falwell to the high court.

While structuring the movie, we realized we couldn't avoid the bane of biopics: the composite character. We got stuck with two. Every time Larry had a major trial, he had different lawyers. And the *Hustler* staffs were fired so often, the masthead was a round-robin of names. The lawyer and the editor were important characters for us, and changing them every ten pages would only confuse the audience. So they became composites.

The editor, Arlo, was easy—a created character based upon a few different guys. As for the lawyer—we knew the movie would end at the Supreme Court. Alan Isaacman was the brilliant attorney who made the passionate winning argument. It seemed absurd to change his name, since it was such a famous case. So working backward, he became the movie lawyer. We incorporated his personality into the overall conception of the part.

While writing the script, the free speech arguments remained amazingly topical. Congress was fighting over the V-chip while also attempting to censor the Internet. The issues don't go away. We had to craft our story so the audience would see our point of view. Fortunately, the bad guys in Larry Flynt's life were like 1980s supervillains: Jerry Falwell, Charles Keating, Ronald Reagan...three powerful men who grabbed a lot of power and alienated a lot of people. With Keating in particular, the ironies were beautiful: He ran a group promoting decency while later garnering fame for bankrupting our country.

After six months of writing, we had a 215-page draft. We cut it down to a brisk 167 and turned it in. (That's sarcasm—scripts normally shouldn't run over 120 pages.) The script was extremely offbeat, and ridiculously over-long, but the studio was hugely supportive.

Then, the real Larry Flynt surfaced. We always knew his curiosity would get the better of him, and he would come knockin'. Technically, we did not need his permission to make the movie. After *Ed Wood* we were experts on what you can and cannot say about a public figure. But with a living person, their contributions can be helpful—plus...a signed release never hurt anyone.

So, a meeting was set up with him. We were terrified—scared of Larry and scared of what he'd think of our script. But when we finally shook hands, it was a shock. He wasn't the fearsome, driven wild man from 1975. Years of medical problems and drugs had mellowed him—he was simply a charming, soft-spoken man in a wheelchair. Regarding the script, his response was com-pletely unpredictable. He liked it, but focused on a rather perplexing matter: How the hell did we learn so much about him?! We shrugged and smiled. Oddly, Larry was okay with us including many embarrassing incidents from his life. His script complaints instead wallowed in absurd minutiae—"I would never say 'Jim Dandy.' I never served biscuits and molasses in the club. The Jackie O issue went to three printings, not four. My magazine never depicted bestiality."

On this last claim, we called his bluff. We knew his life better than he did. "Really? What about that grizzly bear pictorial in October '82?"

A pause. Larry's eyes twinkled mischievously. "Ah, that grizzly was just bein' friendly."

The meeting ended on good terms. Obviously, our script had taken much dramatic license—real life and movies have nothing to do with each other. Yet Larry was smart enough to grasp why events and people were flipped around, deleted, or changed. He intuitively got the game and wasn't going to stop progress. As we were leaving, he smiled at us: "I don't think anybody in the world could've written a better movie about me than you two guys."

We considered this the supreme compliment.

At this point, we did another revision, getting the script down into the 140s. But now Oliver Stone was going off to make *Nixon*. So we needed a director. The studio put together lists of names, and we brought up Milos Forman. The immediate response was mockery—the bravado of these writers, thinking they could get Milos Forman! A world-class filmmaker with an incredible track record—six English-language films, and two had won Best Director and Best Picture Oscars! But to say he wasn't prolific was an understatement. That was six films since 1971. (By comparison, Oliver had made that many since 1989.) Milos hadn't even made a film in the '90s. He lived back East on a remote farm and was considered an unreachable pipedream. But we persisted in pushing for him. The tone of our script was tricky, and the one movie that we thought nailed a similar tone was *One Flew Over the Cuckoo's Nest*—funny, sad, touching, dangerous. Finally Milos read it...and surprise, he said yes!

His reasons were highly personal: He grew up in Czechoslovakia, a society where the Nazis and the Communists controlled all speech. His own family had suffered terrible repercussions. Milos was astute enough to know that pornography is always the first step in censorship. First, you get the perverts...then everyone else.

We worked with Milos for a year, honing the script. Many hours were spent in airless, overheated hotel rooms, where we talked about life and he bombarded us with cigar smoke. The windows never opened, and on a few occasions (particularly in July) we thought we might faint. But the lessons were worthwhile. Milos is a very naturalistic filmmaker—and he is uncomfortable with obvious artifice. So he repeatedly acted out the movie for us, playing every part, seeing how it worked. From this process, changes were made. Shorthand, such as cute quick transitions, was eliminated. Obvious political ramrodding, blacks and whites, got lessened. Milos prefers grays, where the audience has to figure things out. He explained his theory of effective propaganda—the Communists were terrible at it, because the message was obvious. When the viewer knows he's being lectured, he ignores it. What Milos did admire were the more subversive artists in Czechoslovakia, who fought the tyranny with subtext.

Next came casting. Milos has a tradition of using non-actors. We used one established movie star, Woody Harrelson, in the lead. But after that, Milos cast people because of their similarities to the actual characters. Thus Courtney Love, an aggressive, opinionated woman with drugs and stripping in her past, played Althea. Donna Hanover, New York Mayor Rudolph Guiliani's wife, got cast as Jimmy Carter's sister. Brett Harrelson, Woody's overshadowed brother, plays Jimmy, Larry's overshadowed brother.

Our casting director, Francine Maisler, found herself swimming in a sea of oddball personalities. Lawyers got cast off Court TV. Federal marshals got to play themselves. Larry's real staffers, bodyguards, and doctor showed up. Francine got in the spirit of things and boldly suggested James Carville. Perfect. He got to be a prosecutor. Finally, in a capper of nonsense, Larry appeared as his own nemesis, a hard-nosed judge.

On set, these people were given much freedom to improvise. The responses varied. *Babe* farmer James Cromwell played the part of Keating verbatim. Courtney went wild. Edward Norton, as Isaacman, did tons of research, then added legal embellishments that we had actually cut from longer drafts.

Thus, there is no "definitive version" of the screenplay. In some scenes, our earlier drafts more closely resemble the movie than the shooting script. For the purposes of this book, we've gone through all the drafts and assembled a Special Edition. We feel that if you're reading this right now, you have a certain obsessive fondness for the movie and don't simply want a transcript. In that case, you could just buy the videotape. When we published the *Ed Wood* screenplay, we included many deleted scenes, and fans told us those were the best parts of the book. They liked the extra goodies. So this volume contains many extra scenes, as well as longer or alternate versions. In the end notes, we will explain how the film changed from original script, to shooting script, to dailies, to final cut.

In closing, we need to thank three people who took risks and got this unusual film made. At Columbia Pictures, Lisa Henson and Michael Costigan were there for us all along. They never shirked from the subject matter, never second-guessed, never lost faith. And we also owe Janet Yang, our producer and Oliver's partner. She fought hard, getting it from development deal to finished movie without compromises. And the elapsed time from pitch to release was only three years, shockingly fast in studio time.

There were a thousand reasons not to make this movie. We're grateful to those who said "yes."

"THE PEOPLE VS. LARRY FLYNT"

by

Scott Alexander & Larry Karaszewski

FADE IN:

EXT. APPALACHIA - DAY

Eastern Kentucky, 1952. The land is dusty, brown, ferociously
unpromising.

A little boy appears above a hill. He is chunky, barefoot,
with freckles and a puff of red hair. This is LARRY FLYNT, all
of 10 years old. Larry is backwoods, dirt poor, barely
educated, yet bursting with Huckleberry Finn industriousness.

Larry tugs a wooden cart loaded with JUGS. He drags it around
a curve in the lane, coming upon a group of MEN sitting on
logs. They are <u>literally</u> hillbillies: No teeth, foul-looking,
disturbingly inbred.

                    HILLBILLY
          Finally! Sun's goin' down, boy.

                    LARRY
          Keep yer pants on. It's worth the
          wait.
                    (he dramatically uncorks a jug)
          Now today -- I'm askin' a nickel a
          bottle, or two bits a jug.

                    HILLBILLY
                    (shocked)
          "Two BITS"?!

                    LARRY
          Yeah yeah, I know that's pricy...
          but take my word -- this is the
          harshest sauce you done ever drank.

A few glances, then the leader hesitantly buys a bottle. He
guzzles the brew thirstily -- then GASPS, overwhelmed.

                                        CUT TO:

EXT. LOG CABIN - DAY

The Flynt family home is a pitiful, crumbling log cabin in a
field. Larry jauntily strides up, pulling his empty wagon.

Suddenly younger, less-clever brother JIMMY runs out, panicked.

                    JIMMY
          Larry, Larry, come quick! Pa found
          the still!!

                    LARRY
          Aw Christ!

Larry and Jimmy hurriedly run behind the house.

Back in the woods is a tin shed. They whip open the door --
and inside is grizzled PA FLYNT, sucking on a rubber tube
coming out of a moonshine still.

> LARRY
> HEY! What're you doin' in here?!!

> PA FLYNT
> (startled)
> You leave me alone!

> LARRY
> I told ya, I make that for peddlin'!

> PA FLYNT
> I'm your father. You show me some
> respect!

Larry snaps. He suddenly grabs an empty jug and CRACKS it over
Pa's head.

SMASH! Pa goes down.

Jimmy is stunned.

> JIMMY
> Oh no.

Pa staggers up, livid.

> PA FLYNT
> You're gonna pay...!

OUTSIDE

Their MOTHER steps out on the front porch.

> MA FLYNT
> Supper's ready!

Suddenly -- BAM! BAM!

Larry and Jimmy come running for their lives, followed by Pa
SHOOTING his rifle.

Ma shakes her head: Boys will be boys.

The kids disappear into the woods. Pa stumbles a few more
feet, then passes out.

3   IN THE WOODS   3

Larry and Jimmy dash through the trees.

> JIMMY
> Why you always antagonizin' people?!

                    LARRY
          S'matter of principle. He was
          drinkin' my profits.

Exhausted, Larry stops and flops down on the cool grass.

                    LARRY
          I can't wait to grow up and get outta
          here.

                    JIMMY
          Yeah. Then we can go work in the
          coal mines.

                    LARRY
                (he frowns)
          I ain't wastin' my life in no coal
          mine. I wanna be rich.
                (beat)
          I'm leavin' Appalachia.

                    JIMMY
          That's crazy talk. God put us here
          for a reason.

Larry solemnly shakes his head.

                    LARRY
          You're wrong, Jimmy. God wants us
          to make somethin' of our lives.
                (sincere)
          That's why he created the USA. He's
          givin' us a chance. It's the only
          country in the world where anybody
          can be a success.

                                        CUT TO:

SUPER: "20 YEARS LATER"

A pair of pasty-covered tits get shaken in our face.

It's Columbus, Ohio, 1972. And we're in...

4   INT. HUSTLER LOUNGE - NIGHT   4

A rowdy party rocks under a banner, "Hustler Club #8 -- Now
Open!" This go-go bar is a tacky, poor man's version of a
Playboy Club: Waitresses in bikinis, pool tables, black velvet
paintings of nudes, and ROCKABILLY MUSIC. The CROWD is dressy
white trash. They hoot and hollar as the STRIPPER shimmies her
stuff. Finally she removes her pasties, and the song ends.

The stripper exits, and LARRY pats her ass and jumps onto the
tiny stage. Not much has changed: He's now 30, but still
chunky, freckled, and hugely ambitious. Larry's spent his life
trying to improve himself, yet he'll never transcend his
impulsive, crude Kentucky roots. He grins, having a helluva
good time.

                         LARRY
          Thank you! Ain't she somethin'?!
          Ain't this a party?! Am I not
          bringin' you the finest tail in
          southern Ohio???

The crowd CHEERS. Larry beams.

                         LARRY
          And they said it couldn't be done!
          Eight clubs in three years. If you
          haven't joined up, lifetime
          memberships are still available, for
          ten dollars. That entitles you to
          our backroom swinger parties,
          complimentary limousine service,
          half-price well drinks, and starting
          today... a ten-cent luncheon buffet!

More cheers.

Suddenly -- CRASH!

                         VOICE
          You son bitch!

Everyone turns. It's a brawl. TWO REDNECKS punch each other
at the pool table.

Larry frowns. He shouts.

                         LARRY
          Jimmy! You sleepin' back there?
          These gentlemen need assistance.

AT THE BAR

is grown-up JIMMY, bartending. He nods dimly.

Jimmy reaches under the counter and pulls out a LEAD PIPE. He
strides over to the fighters.

                         JIMMY
          Fuckin' hicks. Show a little class!

Jimmy starts wailing on them with the pipe. Crack! Smack!
Blood gushes from their heads. Jimmy efficiently grabs the two
guys under his arms and throws them out the door.

A beat -- then the crowd APPLAUDS. Wow. That's entertainment.

ANGLE - LARRY

He stares at this odd mob behavior, then shrugs and plays
along.

                              LARRY
                    The Hustler Club! Where somethin's
                    always happening!!

                                                  CUT TO:

5   LATE THAT NIGHT   5

    The club is closed. Larry sits at a table with an adding
    machine and cashbox, quietly going over receipts.

    Jimmy sweeps up.

                              JIMMY
                    What a night, huh? We sure packed
                    'em in!

                              LARRY
                         (deadpan)
                    We're broke.

                              JIMMY
                    Say what?!

                              LARRY
                    The giveaways are eating up our
                    profits. It's costing us too much
                    money to get the customers through
                    the door.

                              JIMMY
                         (confused)
                    But, people like the smorgasbord.

                              LARRY
                    That ain't the point. They don't
                    come here to eat. They come here to
                    see titty.

    Jimmy nods. The strippers walk up, now in street clothes.

                              STRIPPER #1
                    Larry, we're ready to go.

                              LARRY
                    Okay.
                         (as they file past, he comments
                          and pays each girl a TWENTY)
                    Nice work... I liked your routine
                    tonight... I'll stop over in an
                    hour... hey, good job... I've never
                    seen a candle blown out that way...
                    bye bye...

    The girls leave. Larry watches them.

IN THE DOORWAY

The strippers sashay out, their curvy bodies silhouetted in the neon lights outside.

ON LARRY AND JIMMY

Larry is entranced.

> LARRY
> Look at those jugs... look at that ass! Man, if I could just advertise what great lays those girls are, we'd be packed every night!

> JIMMY
> Yeah, well no newspaper is gonna print that.

Hmm. Larry thinks...

                                              CUT TO:

6   INT. PRINTSHOP - DAY   6

A greasy printshop. A FRIENDLY OLD PRINTER behind the counter talks to Larry.

> PRINTER
> A promotional newsletter, huh? Well, let me show you examples of some others we've done: The YMCA, the Gardening Club --

> LARRY
> That's alright. I've got my own artwork.

Larry pulls out a handful of black-and-white PHOTOS of topless women. He casually spreads them on the counter.

The old printer is shocked.

> PRINTER
> Whew! This stuff is pretty strong.
> (beat)
> Mister, what kind of business is this?

> LARRY
> I run the Hustler go-go clubs. I'm sure you've heard of them.

> PRINTER
> (confused)
> Mm... no...

Larry shrugs.

                    LARRY
          Well that's why I need the
          newsletter!
                    (beat)
          So I was thinkin' we'd do maybe ten,
          twelve pages an issue.

                    PRINTER
                    (worried)
          With nothing but nudie pictures?

                    LARRY
          Yeah! And I thought we could do it
          on that nice, smooth paper --

                    PRINTER
          That's called slick. But... I could
          get in trouble for printing these
          pictures. There's laws! You gotta
          have some sort of text.

                    LARRY
                    (bewildered)
          Why?

                    PRINTER
          Because! To keep it from being
          called obscene, you gotta have
          ideas... anything... something about
          something.
                    (beat)
          Writing.

Larry thinks.

                    LARRY
          Okay. We'll do a joke page.

                                        CUT TO:

7   EXT. HUSTLER LOUNGE - DAY   7

BLUENOSE PICKETERS walk in circles outside Larry's club.

                    PICKETERS
          No more smut! No more smut!

A car screeches up. Larry hops out, waving a pile of "HUSTLER"
NEWSLETTERS. He cheerily hands them out.

                    LARRY
          Anybody need our new schedule? I
          thought you'd wanna know that Patty's
          doin' her hot sausage number Friday
          night.

The picketers are repulsed.

                              PICKETER
                    <u>God punishes the wicked!</u>

Larry chuckles. He goes inside.

8   INT. HUSTLER LOUNGE - SAME TIME   8

The bar is half-filled. A bored stripper is going through her
motions. At the luncheon buffet, Larry grabs some baloney and
white bread.

Onstage, the COUNTRY-WESTERN SONG ends. The stripper exits, to
scattered applause.

Suddenly -- POUNDING ROCK 'N ROLL. People look up. The
curtains part, and a wild young woman in hot pants and halter
top strides out. She is crazed, shaking with the rhythms,
having a blast. 17 years going on 35, this is the woman who's
going to change Larry's life. Her name is ALTHEA LEASURE.

LARRY

glances up, startled, sandwich frozen in his mouth. What the?!

ALTHEA

struts across stage. Waif-like, strangely pretty, she is a
compelling pile of contradictions: Driven, kinky, desperate for
love, tempered with small-town ignorance and innocence. She
teasingly removes her top.

LARRY

slowly swallows. He waves over Jimmy.

                         LARRY
               Jimmy, who is that?

                         JIMMY
               New girl. I hired her last week.
                    (admiring her)
               She really moves, don't she?

                         LARRY
               She sure does...
                    (he squints)
               but she ain't eighteen.

                         JIMMY
               Course she is -- I saw her I.D.

                         LARRY
                    (annoyed)
               You idiot, my fuckin' <u>dog</u> can get
               I.D.
                    (beat)
               Don't even know why I keep you around
               here.
                         (more)

                              LARRY (Cont'd)
          Look -- when she's done takin' off
          her clothes... you send her up to my
          office.

                                             CUT TO:

9   LARRY'S OFFICE - MINUTES LATER   9

    Up in his spartan office, Larry peeks down through a small
    window. We hear the SAME SONG reaching its climax. Larry's
    eyes are wide -- he can't take 'em off the stage. Finally the
    MUSIC ENDS, to raucous applause.

    Larry quickly shuts the window. He runs behind his desk,
    straightens his jacket, and composes himself. Larry waits.
    Finally -- KNOCK KNOCK!

    Althea peeks in. She's back in street clothes.

                              ALTHEA
          You wanted to see me, Sir?

                              LARRY
                    (surprised)
          "Sir"?? Now I know you're under
          eighteen! Nobody's called me "Sir"
          in my entire life!
                    (beat)
          Honey, an underage creampuff like you
          could cost me my liquor license.

                              ALTHEA
                    (nervously acting tough)
          I'm legal. Here.

    Althea whips out a DRIVER'S LICENSE and tosses it over.

    THE LICENSE - is pathetically fake. The name says "Jane
    Smith," and the birthdate is smudged and liquid-papered over.

    Larry CHORTLES merrily.

                              LARRY
          And this fooled my brother?! Jesus
          Christ is he stupid!

                              ALTHEA
                    (insulted)
          Hey, it's fooled lots of people.
          I've danced in clubs all over town.

    Larry stares at her.

                              LARRY
          So how old are ya?

                              ALTHEA
          Sevente -- uh, seventeen and a half.

                    LARRY
          What does your family think... that
          you strip for a livin'?

                    ALTHEA
          My family's dead.
                    (beat)
          What does your family think, that you
          PAY girls to strip for a livin'?

She smiles devilishly. He raises an eyebrow.

                    LARRY
          They think, "Larry, as long as you
          keep sendin' us those nice checks,
          we'll keep our fuckin' mouths shut"!

Larry laughs. Althea laughs too.

                    ALTHEA
          You got a cute smile.

                    LARRY
                    (startled)
          Er... thank you, Jane.

                    ALTHEA
          Eh, the I.D.'s total bullshit. My
          name's Althea.
                    (she grins)
          So... I hear you balled all the girls
          in the club. Is that true?

                    LARRY
          Most rumors are.

                    ALTHEA
          So how come you haven't tried to ball
          me?

Larry leans forward, impressed. This chick is something.

                    LARRY
          Well, gee, Althea... I only met ya
          three minutes ago.

                                        CUT TO:

10 OUTSIDE LARRY'S OFFICE - LATER   10

Jimmy walks past, eating a sandwich. Inside the door, he hears
SOUNDS OF CRAZED, INTENSE FUCKING.

Jimmy stops, dumbfounded. He shakes his head.

                    JIMMY
          How's he do it?! Fires a girl and
          fucks her at the same time!

                                        DISSOLVE TO:

11 EXT. LOUNGE - LATE NIGHT   11

The neon "Hustler" sign turns off.

12 INT. LOUNGE - SAME TIME   12

Larry's door is <u>still</u> closed. Jimmy POUNDS on it.

                    JIMMY
          Larry! Closin' time.

                    LARRY'S VOICE
                    (distracted)
          Ehhh... okay! Just leave the keys.
          I'll lock up.

                    JIMMY
          But we were gonna stop at the night
          deposit, with the receipts --

                    LARRY'S VOICE
          JIMMY, GET THE FUCK OUTTA HERE! GO!
          ...AND DON'T LOSE THE MONEY!

Jimmy looks hurt. He marches off.

13 INSIDE THE OFFICE   13

The place is totally disheveled. Everything is knocked down.
Larry and Althea are sweaty and naked, half-on half-off a sofa
bed. Larry pants exhaustedly. Althea climbs on him.

                    ALTHEA
          C'mon Larry, one more fuck.

                    LARRY
                    (overwhelmed)
          Baby, be reasonable! Even Superman
          has his limits.

Althea shakes her head.

                    ALTHEA
          See, this is why women are superior.
          Their batteries don't run down.

                    LARRY
          So go fuck a woman.

                    ·ALTHEA
          I do.

Larry does a take.

                         LARRY
          Excuse me?

                         ALTHEA
                  (she grins wickedly)
          You're not the only one that's had
          every girl in this club.

Larry is amazed.

                                        CUT TO:

14   INT. COFFEE SHOP - DAY   14

In a dirty diner, Larry eats breakfast with Jimmy. Larry
excitedly shovels eggs and grits into his mouth.

                         LARRY
          This chick is unbelievable! She's
          a _monster_. I've never met anyone
          more perverted than me!

                         JIMMY
                  (incredulous)
          So one night, and she's movin' in
          with you??

                         LARRY
          What can I do?! Ever since she
          escaped from the orphanage, she's got
          nowhere to stay.

                         JIMMY
          Orphanage?!

                         LARRY
                  (pouring Tabasco on his food)
          Yeah. Her daddy went buggy, shot her
          mama, her grandparents, a bunch of
          other folks, then blew his own brains
          out! Althea's all fucked up.
                  (he chews)
          I thought she could use a break.

Suddenly a BIG-BELLIED TRUCKER lopes up, grinning.

                         TRUCKER
          Hey! Aren't you the guy in that
          little sex paper?

                         LARRY
                  (surprised)
          Uh, yeah. How can I help ya?

                         TRUCKER
          Well hang on a minute! I got some
          naked pictures of my wife out in the
          truck -- I think they'd be perfect
          for your next issue.

Larry is bewildered.

                    LARRY
          Look, it's not a community bulletin
          board. I run photos of my dancers,
          to promote the clubs.

                    TRUCKER
          What clubs?

                    LARRY
          The Hustler strip bars.

                    TRUCKER
               (he shrugs)
          Never heard of 'em. I found the
          paper in a gas station restroom. But
          I just <u>love</u> the pictures! How do I
          subscribe?

Larry looks up. Hmm! An idea is percolating inside his head.

15   EXT. NEWSSTAND - DAY   15

Larry strolls down a street, totally preoccupied. He glances
at a newsstand, then notices a stack of "Playboys." A beat --
then Larry walks back.

                    LARRY
          Hey, gimme one of those Playboys.

                                        CUT TO:

16   INT. LARRY'S APARTMENT - DAY   16

Larry's apartment is a small plasterboard one-bedroom affair.
His BLUE COLLAR FRIENDS are over for Sunday football, rowdily
CHEERING the TV. Althea walks in, with a tray of snacks.

                    ALTHEA
          Here ya go, boys. Try to keep the
          dip off the carpet.

They grab the food. One of them takes a pen and starts drawing
a rude cartoon on a paper plate. He giggles. This is CHESTER,
a moronic, stunningly crude hick.

                    CHESTER
          Hey guys, look. He's got "foot
          balls"!
               (he waves the drawing)
          Get it? His balls are shaped like
          foots!

Everyone looks at the stupid cartoon and LAUGHS.

Larry sits in back, glaring at his Playboy. Althea leans over,
smiling, and gives him a soul kiss. She admires the
centerfold.

                         ALTHEA
          Mmm, nice ass.

                         LARRY
          Of course it's nice! It's all been
          painted over. Don't even look real!
                    (very irritated)
          I just don't understand nothin' about
          this magazine. Ten pages of fuzzy
          photos, and articles about I don't
          know what the hell they're talkin'
          about!
                    (to his friends)
          Hey, you guys read Playboy, don't ya?

                         FRIENDS
                    (adlib)
          Yeah! Sure! You bet! It's the
          greatest!!

                         LARRY
          Did you enjoy this month's article
          about hooking up your own
          quadraphonic sound system?

The guys scratch their heads.

                         FRIEND #1
          Uh... no, Larry. I skipped that one.

                         LARRY
                    (bitterly sarcastic)
          Oh. Well did you follow the advice
          on how to fix a perfect martini?

The guys glance unsurely at the BEER BOTTLES in their hands.

                         LARRY
          And looky here! Porsche was named
          "Car of the Year." Again! Jimmy,
          what're you drivin' these days?

                         JIMMY
                    (baffled)
          Larry, you know I drive a '65 GM
          pickup.

Larry angrily flips through the magazine.

                         LARRY
          Yeah, right. And then there's the
          world famous Playboy Interview!
          Chester, did you read the interview
          with Alan Jay Lerner?

                         CHESTER
          Umm... no, Larry.

                         LARRY
          Do you know who Alan Jay Lerner is?

                        CHESTER
                        (ashamed)
               Umm... no, Larry.

CLOSEUP - LARRY

He's at the boiling point.

                         LARRY
               This is what I'm talkin' about! Who
               is this magazine for?! Says here
               they got a circulation of seven
               million! Seven million people a
               month buyin' it, and not a single
               person knows what they're reading!!
                        (livid)
               Gentlemen, PLAYBOY IS MOCKING YOU!!!

WIDE

The room is deadly quiet. A glum beat.

                      TV ANNOUNCER
               I don't believe it! He makes the
               kick!! The Bengals WIN!!!!!!!

The guys stare silently at the TV. They missed the win.

                                           CUT TO:

17   INT. BANK - DAY   17

Larry grins ebulliently in a cheap polyester three-piece suit.
He's bulldozing a bespectacled, disturbed LOAN OFFICER.

                         LARRY
               It'll be HUGE! All pictures topless
               bottomless. No punches pulled. The
               first magazine for Joe Lunchbox...
               for our people!

                      LOAN OFFICER
               Our people??
                        (uncomfortable)
               Mr. Flynt... do you know how
               difficult it is to start a magazine?
               You need writers, photographers, a
               whole talent pool... I'm not aware
               of one national publication run out
               of Ohio --

> LARRY
> It don't matter. We'll be small, but
> a lean machine!
> (he lowers his voice)
> See, here's the deal. I run enough
> bars that I can buy Schoenling Beer
> at below wholesale. So I'm gonna
> quietly lay off sixty cases a month
> on the paper manufacturer. In
> return, he's gonna slip me the paper
> at half-price, provided I do the
> typesetting at the printshop owned
> by his brother.

The loan officer is overwhelmed.

> LOAN OFFICER
> Look, Mr. Flynt, this is all quite
> fascinating. But I'm afraid --

> LARRY
> Please! There's no risk for you.
> I'm willin' to put my neck on the
> line! I'll take all my clubs, my
> car, everything I own and use 'em to
> secure the loan!

> LOAN OFFICER
> (he shakes his head)
> I'm sorry. Our bank's just not
> interested.

A tense moment -- then unrelenting Larry pulls out a photo of a
GORGEOUS BLONDE.

> LARRY
> What if I brought in Blowjob Bambi
> to close the deal?

The loan officer gulps.

                                        CUT TO:

18   EST. BRICK BUILDING - DAY   18

A low-rent, crumbling number. A hand-painted sign says
"Hustler Magazine."

19   INT. MAGAZINE OFFICES - DAY   19

The first day. In junky offices, Althea, Jimmy, Chester, and a
few long-haired, rebel STAFFERS work at bridge tables. One guy
sloppily assembles a page mock-up with scotch tape.

> STAFFER
> Do we type the numbers on the pages,
> or will the printer do it for us?

People shrug.

In a corner is a hippie, ARLO CASEY, a high i.q., sardonic underachiever. He smokes a joint and flips through naked pictures.

> ARLO
> Man, this sure beats interning at the Free Press.

20   IN A BACK ROOM   20

is a photo shoot. Against bare concrete, a groovy black photographer, RUDY, arranges a naked MODEL on a bed. Larry watches impatiently.

> RUDY
> Baby, try holding the flower in your right hand. No... put it in your left. Nah, that ain't no good. Try it against the satin sheet.

> LARRY
> For Christ's sake, Rudy, I don't give a shit about sheets and flowers! All we're selling is the girl! Now c'mon.

Larry strides behind the tripod and peers through the CAMERA. Suddenly, he frowns.

> LARRY
> HEY. What is wrong with this camera??! It's all murky!

> RUDY
> Yeah, that's a trick of the trade. It's vaseline on the lens -- it makes the girls soft and pretty.

> LARRY
> (freaking out)
> Why would you want that?! It's dishonest!

> RUDY
> (unnerved)
> B-but, uh, it's dreamy. Like a fantasy --

> LARRY
> Why d'ya need to fantasize?! You got a real naked woman here! Look how good she looks.

> MODEL
> Why thank you, Mr. Flynt.

Larry glances at her. Suddenly he gets a look.

                    LARRY
          In fact... Rudy, why don't you take
          a thirty-minute break and let her and
          me get acquainted...?

                    RUDY
               (warily)
          Aw, c'mon, Larry! I already got my
          equipment set-up and everything.

                    LARRY
          Oh, fine.
               (pouting)
          Well, do it, then.

Rudy nods. He gets behind the camera and starts CLICKING shots
of the girl.

                    RUDY
          Okay baby, that's great!
               (CLICK)
          That's nice! Yeah, a little more
          arm.
               (CLICK)
          Now spread your legs. A little
          wider...
               (CLICK)
          A little wider...
               (CLICK)
          A little wider... OOPS! That's a
          little too wide. Uh, you better put
          that back in --

                    LARRY
          NO! WAIT A SECOND. That was GOOD!
               (wide-eyed)
          Do it again!

Rudy is flustered. He stops shooting.

                    RUDY
          B-but, Larry... you can't show
          that...

                    LARRY
          Why not?! God made the genitals --
          who are we to say they aren't
          beautiful??

Rudy grimaces.

                                        CUT TO:

21   INT. HUSTLER OFFICES - DAY   21

Staffers hold photo SLIDES up to a bright window. They gawk in
disbelief.

                    ARLO
          These are gonna blow people's minds!

                    STAFFER
          We're not really runnin' these??

                    LARRY
          Sure we are. The vagina has as much
          personality as the face.
                    (beat)
          We wanna make a nice impression on
          our inaugural issue.

Arlo LAUGHS crazily. Chester shuffles in, holding a phone.

                    CHESTER
          Larry, I got the printer on the line.
          He says to do my cartoons, I gotta
          supply him with a color separation.

                    LARRY
          Yeah...?

                    CHESTER
          So what is a color separation?

Hmm.

Everybody glances around. No answers.

                    LARRY
          Gimme that phone.
                    (into receiver)
          Look Bo, don't bother my creative
          staff with these technical questions.
          They're very busy. You just get
          those 200,000 copies out on the
          street.

Larry angrily HANGS UP.

                                        CUT TO:

22 EXT. NEWSSTAND - DAY   22

A delivery truck pulls up, and the driver tosses out a pile of
"HUSTLER" magazines! The old codger NEWS DEALER cuts open the
pile, then thumbs through the top issue.

Suddenly -- he freezes in horror.

                    NEWS DEALER
          Jesus Christ.

The man quickly hides the magazines up on the top shelf.

                                        CUT TO:

23   INT. HUSTLER OFFICES - DAY   23

Rudy's model is now working as a Hustler secretary. She
answers the phone.

                    SECRETARY
          Hustler Magazine. Think pink.

A door opens, and Larry scoots in, carrying a bakery box. He
hurries past the staffers and bounces up to Althea. He beams.

                    LARRY
          Happy birthday, baby!

He pops open the box. Inside is a BIRTHDAY CAKE: It has a
jolly plastic naked girl and the message, "YOU'RE 18! JAILBAIT
NO MORE!" But Althea doesn't even smile.

Larry looks about. Everybody is gloomy-faced.

                    LARRY
          What?

                    ARLO
          The distributor called. We only got
          a 25-percent sellthrough.

                    LARRY
          Which means...?

                    JIMMY
          Which means they're sendin' back
          150,000 copies!

Larry collapses in a chair.

                    LARRY
          Oh shit.

                    JIMMY
               (panicked)
          Larry, we're practically wiped out!

Larry's face goes ashen.

                                             CUT TO:

24   INT. LARRY'S OFFICE - DAY   24

Larry lies on a ratty couch, staring glumly at the ceiling.
Althea sits with him.

                    LARRY
          I'm so stupid. Why'd I ever think
          I could pull this off?!
               (beat)
          I'm just a fuckin' hillbilly...!

> ALTHEA
> Aw c'mon, honey -- cheer up. Look!

Althea tugs the little naked lady off the cake and teasingly licks her crotch.

Larry can't laugh. So she consolingly puts her arms around him.

> ALTHEA
> At least ya tried. You got balls.

> LARRY
> But I don't got the smarts!
> (terribly upset)
> It's <u>over</u>. Another couple issues, and we're in the poorhouse.

> ALTHEA
> So what. Being poor ain't so bad.

> LARRY
> (enraged)
> It sure fuckin' is! <u>I'm not goin' back</u>! I spent my childhood watchin' my mama cry, cause I didn't have shoes to go to school.
> (beat)
> Never again.

AT THE DOOR

Arlo enters.

> ARLO
> Hey Larry, I got a guy on the phone, callin' from Italy. Says he's got naked pictures of Jackie O.

> LARRY
> (scoffing)
> Yeah, right.

> ARLO
> I dunno... claims he already went to "Playboy" and "Penthouse," but they said the photos were too tasteless.

Hmm?! Larry perks up.

25   INT. LARRY'S OFFICE - LATER   25

Larry is on the phone, listening to a HEAVILY-ACCENTED JOVIAL ITALIAN MAN.

                    ITALIAN MAN (v.o.)
          I was on-a that old fishink boat,
          watchin' the island of Skorpios for
          four months! For <u>four months</u> I
          rented that telephoto lens...
          waiting, waiting... but the Jackie
          O. never come out.
                    (very dramatic)
          And then-a one day, the cabana door
          opens -- and Mama Mia! -- out comes
          the Jackie O. in the raw!

                    LARRY
          So what do you see??

                    ITALIAN MAN (v.o.)
                    (he laughs)
          You see <u>everything</u>, my friend!!

Larry is starstruck. He GASPS.

                    LARRY
          Jesus Christ.
                    (beat)
          First Pussy!

                    ITALIAN MAN (v.o.)
          And she's the good one! This ain't-a
          no Mamie Eisenhower or Lady Bird.

Larry shakes with excitement.

                                        CUT TO:

26   INT. PRINTING PRESSES - DAY   26

Magazines fly out of rumbling printing presses. A blur of
colorful paper rushes by.

                                        CUT TO:

27   INT. NEW YORK SUBWAY STATION - NIGHT   27

A train pulls in. The doors open, and 100 MIDDLE CLASS JOES
trudge off, end of the day. The mob passes a newsstand. A
banner hangs: "AUGUST HUSTLER: JACQUELINE KENNEDY ONASSIS
NUDE!"

A beat.

Suddenly, <u>everyone</u> stops and looks back. The crowd is stunned.
They stare -- then suddenly STORM the newsstand. Guys are
knocking each other over, trying to get at the magazines first.

                                        CUT TO:

28   INT. HUSTLER OFFICES - DAY   28

Salesmen scream into a bank of phones.

                    SALESMAN #1
        You want another three hundred -- oh
        -- you want another three <u>thousand</u>
        copies!?

                    SALESMAN #2
        Yeah, we're doing a fourth printing!
        But not till Friday!
            (beat)
        WHAT? Huh?! My God -- Larry, turn
        on Channel Ten!!!

29   INT. LARRY'S OFFICE   29

Staffers frantically run in. They gather around a little TV.

ON THE TV

A svelte REPORTER stands in front of the Ohio Statehouse.

                    REPORTER (on TV)
        ...everyone's talking about local boy
        done good -- or bad -- Larry Flynt,
        whose Hustler magazine has reached
        national sales of an astonishing two
        million copies.
            (beat)
        Well in a stunning disclosure,
        WBNS-TV has learned that Ohio
        Governor Jim Rhodes himself was
        spotted today at a newsstand, buying
        a copy of the infamous Jackie O.
        issue.

THE STAFFERS

go crazy. What?!!!! They're WHOOPING, HOLLERING in disbelief.

ON THE TV

White-haired GOVERNOR RHODES appears. He looks nervous and
confused.

                    GOVERNOR RHODES (on TV)
        Well, er, uh... everybody knows I've
        been a historical buff on First
        Ladies for a long time.

THE STAFFERS

SCREAM happily and LAUGH their heads off. People smack Larry
on the back. He grins, flabbergasted and proud.

                                CUT TO:

30   INT. BANQUET ROOM - NIGHT   30

A roomful of CONSERVATIVE MEN AND WOMEN. Up front, a hawklike
TALL MAN speaks authoritatively.

                         TALL MAN
          What is a community? A community is
          a collection of people, things, and
          ideas which interact to form a way
          of life. A teacher educates our
          youth, and they become model
          citizens. The clergyman preaches,
          and we find spirituality. My bank
          gives loans, and homes get built.
                    (an ominous pause)
          But NOW... there is a new, darker
          influence in Cincinnati. Mr. Leis,
          if you would?

SIMON LEIS, the sour, spooky Hamilton County Prosecutor, pulls
out a pile of Hustlers. He starts passing them out to
everyone.

People are shocked.

                         LEIS
          Ladies and Gentlemen, please examine
          these materials carefully. Because
          they were not purchased in some dirty
          bookstore. I bought them myself, in
          a neighborhood grocery -- in plain
          sight!

One lady covers her eyes. The Tall Man threateningly waves the
Hustler in her face.

                         TALL MAN
          Ma'am, you cannot hide from this!
          Good people are being corrupted!
          Why, just look what happened to our
          fine Governor!
                    (he shakes his head)
          As members of the Citizens for Decent
          Literature, we can not relent! We
          must prevent the destruction of the
          soul of our country.

Everybody APPLAUDS.

A beat -- then we PUSH IN to a nametag on the man's lapel. It
says "Hello, my name is Charles Keating."

                                              CUT TO:

31 INT. LARRY'S OFFICE - LATE NIGHT   31

Six FRAMED Hustler magazines hang proudly on the wall.

Larry works at a bulletin board, arranging page mockups for the
next issue. Althea sits at a table, totaling receipts on the
old adding machine. She punches in numbers -- then suddenly
gets an odd expression. The TOTAL is $1,001,205.

Althea's eyes widen.

> ALTHEA
> Larry, take off your pants.

> LARRY
> Why?

> ALTHEA
> I want to fuck a millionaire..

Larry gasps. Althea laughs joyfully and jumps onto him.

> WIPE TO:

32 EST. TUDOR MANSION - NIGHT   32

A gorgeous tudor mansion stands on a lush green property. A sign says "Flynt Manor."

33 INT. MANSION - SAME TIME   33

A BIG PARTY is rocking. The house is an advertent parody of tasteless nouveau riche. Gurgling founta' animal skins, a black velvet portrait of Larry and Althea it's stroke-inducing decor. A "HAPPY BICENTEN." banner drapes over a lavish fried chicken buffet. Red, te, and blue bunting is everywhere.

Hundreds of PARTYGOERS dance, drink, and rugs. Some are naked and make out. A Japanese MAID serv napes in the commotion. Suddenly -- we HEAR MILITARY-S DRUMMING. Everyone rushes out back to see what's ha ng.

34 OUTSIDE   34

On the lawn, four high-school DRUMMERS mar drill formation. They part -- and Larry strides proudly dressed as a Revolutionary War soldier. He salute crowd.

> LARRY
> Happy Birthday, America!

Fireworks EXPLODE! Everyone cheers. Red, and blue fireworks light up arranged as the American Then another display erupts, depicting two women's nude groping.

Larry beams.

> LARRY
> I put the "bi" back in Bicentenni

People LAUGH.

A SERVANT comes over and whispers something y's ear. Larry lights up even more and runs out thro house.

35   EXT. MANSION - NIGHT   35

     Larry's parents step fom a LIMO, overwhelmed. Aged Pa Flynt
     is in a heavy coat. Smple Ma Flynt clutches her purse. Larry
     runs up and hugs them.

                         LARRY
               Ma! Pa! Y came!

                         MA FLYNT
                    (qut)
               Larry, this ouse is so big...

                         LARRY
               Not bad for cracker with an
               eighth-gra education, eh?!

     Larry escorts them a. A CHAUFFEUR follows with luggage.

36   INT. MANSION   36

     Larry leads his pare in, pushing through the crowd. The
     chauffeur struggles er them.

                         MA FLYNT
               Who are a hese people?

                         LARRY
               My friend
                    (estures)
               So what think?! We got
               servant' rters, library... and
               look! A al dining room --

                         PA FLYNT
                    led)
               "Formal ng room...?

                         LARRY
               Yep! T four rooms in all. You
               know wh has twenty-four rooms?

                         PA FLYNT
               The Pre...?

                         LARRY
               Nah! fner!

                         MA FLYNT
               It's ream. You really made
               it, La

                         LARRY
                    ched)
               Yeah. ne show you your bedroom.

     Larry opens a auses -- then suddenly shuts it.

> LARRY
> Hmm, it's all messy. Hang on a sec'.

Blocking his parents' view, Larry sticks his head back inside.

BEDROOM - SAME TIME

Althea is having sex with TWO NAKED GIRLS.

> LARRY
> Hey, there is a party out here!

> ALTHEA
> (teasing)
> I'm just warmin' them up for you.

Larry glances at the women.

> LARRY
> Oh. Well this is my parents' room.
> Uh... move your buddies to the
> parlor, and I'll see you in ten.

BACK IN THE HALL

Larry quickly shuts the door and palms the chauffeur a HUNDRED.

> LARRY
> Leave the bags here.
> (he grabs his folks)
> C'mon, I wanna show you where Jimmy
> lives.

> PA FLYNT
> Y'know... we appreciate you takin'
> care of your little brother, the way
> you do.

> LARRY
> Of course. He's family.

37   INT. BASEMENT - NIGHT   37

Larry guides Ma and Pa down some dark stairs.

> LARRY
> (mysterious)
> What I got down here is real special.
> I bought a house with an extra-large
> basement, so I'd have room for
> this...

Larry flicks on the LIGHTS.

And sitting in the basement is an exact replica of Larry's childhood home. It's the FLYNTS' KENTUCKY CABIN.

Ma and Pa are flabbergasted.

                         MA FLYNT
            My GOD. Sweet Jesus, look at that..!

                         PA FLYNT
            It's our old house!

                         LARRY
                         (proud)
            It's even got the tar stains on the
            front steps!

                         PA FLYNT
                         (puzzled)
            And this is where Jimmy lives?

Larry LAUGHS heartily.

                         LARRY
            NO! That's a joke.

                         MA FLYNT
            So Larry... why did you build it?

CLOSEUP - LARRY

He smiles sincerely.

                         LARRY
            Ma... I always wanna remember where
            I came from.

Larry gives her a poignant embrace.

                                        DISSOLVE TO:

38   EXT. MANSION YARD - LATE THAT NIGHT   38

The party's over. Litter is everywhere, and the butler and
maid clean up. Across the yard, they hear MOANING. Off in the
dark, submerged in the jacuzzi, is a three-way orgy.

The maid shrugs and continues her business. She clears used
cups off a table -- revealing a pile of cocaine. Oh. She
indifferently scoops it in the trash.

AT THE JACUZZI

In the bubbling water, Larry is screwing a WOMAN from behind.
The woman's head is buried in Althea's crotch. Althea stands
facing Larry, unmoving, staring into his eyes.

Finally, they all orgasm. Pause, and then the woman glides
into the pool and silently swims away.

39   INT. MANSION BEDROOM   39

Ma and Pa Flynt lie on their bed, still dressed. They stare at
the ceiling, totally overwhelmed.

40   BACK IN THE JACUZZI   40

Althea kisses Larry on the nose. He beams.

                    ALTHEA
          That was good.

                    LARRY
          You want a beer?

She shakes her head.

An unsure moment. Althea gulps like a little child.

                    ALTHEA
          Larry... you ever think about gettin'
          married?

                    LARRY
          No.

                    ALTHEA
               (careful, not pushy)
          Why not? Don't you think it shows
          a nice level of commitment...?

                    LARRY
          Nope.
               (he shakes his head)
          See, I was married a lot when I was
          young. I got ex-wives and kids
          scattered all over Ohio. It just
          don't work.

                    ALTHEA
          But --

                    LARRY
          Cause here's the problem: I just
          love poon too much. Different kinds
          of poon. Poon is a glorious thing.
          I can't imagine ever committing to
          just one poon.

Althea is hurt.

                    ALTHEA
          Not even me?

                    LARRY
          Baby, don't get me wrong: You're the
          best. You're the 100-percent finest
          woman I ever met in my life. I'd
          love to be married to you --
               (beat)
          But, my dick runs the show.

Silence, except for the bubbles. Althea is thinking.

                    ALTHEA
          Well... what if it wasn't a problem?
          What if it was okay for you to hump
          whoever you wanted, as long as I knew
          that I was the one you loved?

Larry squirms nervously.

                    LARRY
          Jeez, I dunno, Althea. All of a
          sudden you're really puttin' the
          screws on me.

                    ALTHEA
               (sincere)
          Look, after my parents, I didn't
          think I'd ever want to get married.
          But then I met you.

                    LARRY
               (staring into her eyes)
          So you're really serious...?

                    ALTHEA
          Like a hemorrhoid.

Larry slowly nods, mulling this over.

She waits for a response.

Finally -- he smiles slyly.

                    LARRY
          Ummm, Althea?

                    ALTHEA
               (grinning expectantly)
          Yes, Larry........?

                    LARRY
          Would you be my wife?

Althea SQUEALS happily and hugs him. They kiss excitedly.

                                        CUT TO:

41   MONTAGE - WEDDING STILLS   41

     A montage of stills from a beautiful, traditional ceremony.
     Althea in a white gown. Larry in a 70's tux with fat lapels.
     The bride and groom kissing. Family and friends applaud.

42   INT. MAGAZINE OFFICES - DAY   42

     An editorial meeting. Althea sits alone in a starry-eyed daze,
     transfixed by a sparkling WEDDING RING on her hand.

     At the table, male staffers lustily examine a PHOTO PORTFOLIO
     of a gorgeous brunette.

                    LARRY
          What do ya think? Ain't she hot?

                    ARLO
          Yessir! Totally fuckable!

                    LARRY
          You think so? Okay, turn the page.

They do so. Suddenly -- they all GROAN IN HORROR. AaaahHH!

                    JIMMY
          Oh NO!! She's got a DICK!

                    LARRY
          Heh, heh! Meet our new cover girl!

The group is appalled.

                    STAFFER #1
          Why?! Who would enjoy these
          pictures?

                    LARRY
                (unsure)
          Uh... women.

                    STAFFER #2
          Nah, women wouldn't enjoy them.

                    LARRY
          Okay... men.
                (he shrugs)
          Look, it don't matter. It's like
          when people slow down at a car crash,
          so they can sneak a peek.

                    ARLO
                (he LAUGHS)
          Fuck convention. This magazine dares
          its readers to look.

                    LARRY
          Exactly! We're breakin' taboos like
          Lenny Bruce! So what else y'all got
          for me...?

Larry looks about the room. People think. Finally --

                    JIMMY
          Uh, I know a girl with three nipples.

                    LARRY
          Very good, Jimmy! What else?

                    ARLO
                (deadpan)
          How about a guide to necrophilia?

                         CHESTER
          How about a fifty-year-old
          centerfold?

                         ALTHEA
          How 'bout "The Wizard Of Oz"??

Hmm. Everybody is totally baffled by this suggestion.

                         ARLO
          What do you mean?

                         ALTHEA
          You know, dirty. With the Scarecrow,
          and the Lion, and the Tin Man pullin'
          a train on Dorothy.

The group is shocked.

                         STAFFER #1
          I dunno. There's some things that
          are sacred...

                         LARRY
              (offended)
          Hey, shut up.

                         STAFFER #1
          But Larry, you gotta know where to
          draw the line --

                         LARRY
              (he snaps)
          You're fired! Pack your bags and GET
          OUT! Althea's idea is the best
          fuckin' thing I've heard all day!

Larry and Althea smile at each other.

Suddenly -- the door gets SLAMMED against the wall, and two
POLICE DETECTIVES stride in! They stare grimly.

                         POLICE DETECTIVE
          Larry Claxton Flynt?

                         LARRY
              (puzzled)
          Um, uh... yes?

                         POLICE DETECTIVE
          You're under arrest, on charges of
          pandering obscenity in Cincinnati and
          engaging in organized crime.

They SLAP handcuffs onto Larry. He's dumbfounded.

                                        CUT TO:

43   INT. CINCINNATI JAIL CELL - DAY   43

Larry sits motionless behind bars.

A GUARD walks up, leading a well-dressed man of boyish charm.
This is ALAN ISAACMAN, a sharp, principled lawyer.

                    ISAACMAN
          Mr. Flynt?

                    LARRY
               (leery)
          Who are you?

                    ISAACMAN
          Alan Isaacman. I'm your lawyer.

                    LARRY
          Really...?! Who hired you?

                    ISAACMAN
          Your wife.

                    LARRY
               (impressed)
          Hmm. Is porn your specialty?

Isaacman laughs.

                    ISAACMAN
          I'd like to think not.
               (he smiles)
          But civil liberties are. Do you
          realize what you've stumbled into...?

44   INT. ISAACMAN'S LAWFIRM - DAY   44

A small one-room office. Larry and Althea sit at a desk with
Isaacman.

                    ISAACMAN
          This is war. These guys hate
          pornography, and they're going to use
          you to further their national agenda.

                    LARRY
          Which is what?

                    ISAACMAN
               (grim)
          Censorship.

                    LARRY
          That's ridiculous! I got a right to
          say whatever I want -- uh, don't I?

                    ISAACMAN
          Well, <u>technically</u> the First Amendment
          protects your rights to free speech
          and a free press. But recently,
          individual communities have gone
          haywire imposing their own standards.
          So now what's okay in New York ain't
          okay in Birmingham and sure as hell
          ain't okay in Cincinnati.

Larry gets angry.

                    LARRY
          That's retarded! I can't publish a
          different edition for every city.

                    ISAACMAN
          Exactly. So they're hoping you'll
          take their watered-down version and
          make that the one everyone reads.

This sinks in. Isaacman opens a file.

                    ISAACMAN
          Mr. Flynt, what makes your case odd
          is the organized crime charge.
          They've upped the stakes.

                    ALTHEA
          That's bullshit. He's not in the
          Mob!

                    ISAACMAN
                (eyebrow raised)
          Really, Mr. Flynt?

                    LARRY
          No!

A beat. Larry decides he likes Isaacman.

                    LARRY
          And call me Larry.

                    ISAACMAN
          Okay, Larry. Well, the prosecutors
          are exploiting an obscure Ohio
          statute which says "organized crime"
          is five or more people conspiring in
          an illegal activity.
                (beat)
          The law was passed after Kent State,
          to keep troublemakers from
          assembling.

Isaacman pauses awkwardly.

ISAACMAN
So... if they nail you on the
misdemeanor pandering, it'll turn
into a felony. You're looking at
twenty-five years.

LARRY
Jesus Christ!

The color drains from Larry's face. He slumps back, stunned at
the enormity of this charge.

LARRY
All I'm guilty of is bad taste...!

ALTHEA
(total disbelief)
My cousin Bobby shot a preacher and
only did six months!

ISAACMAN
Well cousin Bobby only hurt one
person. Larry's polluting the minds
of millions.
(back to Larry)
The world thinks you're a pervert in
a raincoat. We're gonna have to
fight back every way we can...

CUT TO:

45   EXT. MANSION - DAY   45

Larry's backyard is filled with a 60 MINUTES CAMERA CREW. They
set-up lights and reflectors by the swimming pool.

Larry hides around the corner, panickedly watching. Isaacman,
Arlo, and Althea are with him.

LARRY
Christ almighty! Why'd I agree to
this? 60 Minutes is gonna eat me
alive!
(he spins around)
Quiz me again.

ISAACMAN
(referring to some notes)
Okay. Tell me about the First
Amendment.

Larry concentrates, furrowing his brow like a schoolkid giving
a speech.

LARRY
"Congress shall make no law reserving"--

                         ARLO
                    (correcting)
          "Respecting."

                         LARRY
          "Uh, <u>respecting</u> an establishment of
          religion, or abridging the freedom
          of speech, or of the press."

Althea CLAPS giddily. Larry breathes a sigh of relief.

                       ISAACMAN
          Good. Okay, give me the Picasso
          line:

                                             CUT TO:

46   LATER   46

The interview. Cameras ROLL on Larry and a CBS NEWSMAN.

                         LARRY
          ...and as Pablo Picasso said, "The
          only true enemy of creativity is good
          taste."
                    (beat)
          See, only two types of people oppose
          pornography. Those that don't know
          what they're talkin' about, or those
          that don't know what they're missing.

The CBS Newsman laughs.

                       CBS NEWSMAN
          In your opinion. This <u>is</u> a
          publication nicknamed "<u>G</u>ynecology
          Today."

                         LARRY
          Look, Moses freed the Jews. Lincoln
          freed the slaves. Lenny Bruce freed
          the dirty word. Larry Flynt would
          just like to free a lot of prudes --

                       CBS NEWSMAN
          And make a lot of money.

                              LARRY
                    That's beside the point.
                         (impassioned)
                    Look, how can a country founded on
                    the printed word, at its 200th
                    birthday, still be questioning what
                    kind of book or movie you can see?!
                    Because when the government
                    interferes in this, they're
                    interfering with our thought process!
                    And nobody has that right.

                                                      CUT TO:

47   INT. LIMO - MORNING   47

      The day of the trial. Charles Keating and Simon Leis sit in a
      limo. Keating reads the New York Times.

                              LEIS
                    Y'know, Charlie, once we convict this
                    guy, we should take it to the
                    Legislature. Toughen the laws.

                              CHARLES KEATING
                         (he nods)
                    I'll help you raise a war chest.

      Keating turns the page -- then GROANS in displeasure. A full
      page newspaper ad screams "LARRY FLYNT: AMERICAN DISSIDENT!"
      Underneath is a petition signed by a hundred names.

                              CHARLES KEATING
                    Oh fudge, the New York bleeding
                    hearts are buttin' in! Listen to
                    this...
                         (irritably reading)
                    "We the undersigned wish to protest
                    the infringement of Mr. Flynt's right
                    under the First Amendment..."

48   INT. TOWNCAR - SAME TIME   48

      Larry and Isaacman read the same ad. Larry is astonished.

                              LARRY
                    "...because it is a threat to the
                    rights of all Americans. Woody
                    Allen! Norman Mailer! Gore
                    Vidal...!"
                         (awestruck, he looks up)
                    Look at these famous people! Does
                    this mean they read Hustler?

                              ISAACMAN
                    No. It means they don't want the
                    government telling us what to do.

49   EXT. CINCINNATI COURTHOUSE - MORNING   49

A series of towncars pull up to the courthouse. As Larry and
his gang stride out, he's surprised by a riled-up SWARM OF
PICKETERS. The two sides hurl ANGRY EPITHETS at each other:
"Remember Sodom and Gomorrah!" "Don't fuck with the Bill of
Rights!" "There's no 'SIN' in Cincinnati!"

Larry marvels at all this.

50   INT. COURTROOM - MORNING   50

The trial. Pudgy JUDGE WILLIAM MORRISSEY presides over the
room. Larry sits at the defendant's table with Isaacman.
Charles Keating and his Decent Citizens watch from the front
row.

Prosecutor Leis addresses the TWELVE JURORS in a heavy
monotone.

                         LEIS
              Good morning, Ladies and Gentlemen.
              Before we begin, I must apologize for
              the dirty, unpleasant task we have
              set before ourselves. But it is
              entirely necessary, to cleanse our
              community of pornographic trash.
                    (he grimaces)
              What you are going to see will take
              your breath away. Hustler depicts
              women and men posed together in a
              lewd and shameful manner. It depicts
              women and women posed together in a
              lewd and shameful manner.
                    (a long beat)
              It even depicts Santa Claus posed in
              a lewd and shameful manner.

The jury GASPS.

AT THE DEFENDANTS

Isaacman leans in and frantically WHISPERS.

                         ISAACMAN
              What's he talking about?

                         LARRY
                    (whispering)
              December '76. Santa takes it up the
              ass.

Isaacman groans.

                         ISAACMAN
              Oh Jesus.

                                             CUT TO:

51   LATER   51

> Isaacman approaches the Judge. A stack of MAGAZINES sits on the evidence table.

                    ISAACMAN
          With the court's permission, at this
          time I'd like to introduce into
          evidence twenty-seven other men's
          magazines widely available in
          Cincinnati. Titles such as Swank,
          Cheri, Players --

                    LEIS
          Objection!

                    ISAACMAN
          Juggs, Gallery --

                    LEIS
          OBJECTION!

                    ISAACMAN
                (barreling ahead)
          These titles have contents virtually
          identical to Hustler, with stories
          on bestiality, incest --

                    JUDGE MORRISSEY
          Mr. Isaacman, what are you driving
          at?

> Isaacman abruptly spreads out the magazines.

                    ISAACMAN
          How can they be legal if Hustler is
          not?? These magazines are sold in
          massive quantities in this city!
          They truly reflect this community's
          level of tolerance.

> The Judge stares.

                    JUDGE MORRISSEY
          No.

                    ISAACMAN
                (startled)
          Excuse me??

                    JUDGE MORRISSEY
          NO. I won't allow these into
          evidence. They're irrelevant to the
          case.

ANGLE - ISAACMAN

> He turns pale.

                    ISAACMAN
        B-but -- Your Honor, they demonstrate
        community standards. They are the
        crux of our argument...

                    JUDGE MORRISSEY
        No, counselor. The jury is
        representative of the community --
        NOT a pile of magazines. You can't
        admit them.

The Judge BANGS his gavel.

Isaacman glowers.

The Decent Citizens smile mysteriously.

52 LATER   52

Larry is on the stand. Leis hounds him, cross-examining.

                    LEIS
        Mr. Flynt, do you imagine that when
        our Founding Fathers wrote the
        Constitution, they envisioned
        charlatans like you exploiting the
        Bill of Rights?

                    LARRY (angry)
        Hey, you can't slice it up! The
        Constitution don't say freedom of the
        press for everybody, except Larry
        Flynt!
                    (beat)
        I've got 10 million readers. That's
        10 million voices that can't be
        ignored! Now we either have a free
        press or we don't!

The jury is fascinated. A SKETCH ARTIST draws Larry.

                    LEIS
        But isn't a community entitled to set
        its own standards?

                    LARRY
        NO, Sir! That's just a disguise for
        "Censorship"! And one of the
        greatest things we have as American
        citizens is the right to be left
        alone. If you don't like Hustler,
        PUT IT DOWN!

                    LEIS
        I do. But what about innocent
        children, when they gaze upon your
        magazine in a grocery?

> LARRY
> Hey! These same places sell booze
> and cigarettes, and we KNOW kids end
> up with those! If a minor got caught
> drinkin' beer in a tavern, would
> Budweiser be banned across the entire
> country??!

53 LATER   53

Isaacman is giving his closing speech.

> ISAACMAN
> Ladies and Gentlemen of the jury:
> Freedom is never lost in one fell
> swoop. Rather, it is eroded little
> by little... one book, one film, one
> newspaper at a time. In the Soviet
> Union, 85 percent of all the
> literature condemned is suppressed
> on obscenity statutes.

He stares each juror in the eye, letting this sink in. Leis
glares.

> ISAACMAN
> Am I proud of Hustler? No, I can't
> say in good conscience that I admire
> everything Hustler says... but I'll
> tell you what I am proud of. I'm
> proud of the fact that I live in a
> country where I can read Hustler if
> I want to, or throw it in the trash
> can. That's what I'm proud of.
>   (very quiet)
> My friends, watch out about building
> walls of decency. Someday, you might
> find the walls have grown up all
> around you.

Isaacman drops his head.

The room is silent.

CLOSEUP - LARRY

His eyes well up with tears. Then, overcome, he bizarrely
starts crying.

CLOSEUP - LEIS

He glowers skeptically. Is Flynt a big put-on?

                                          CUT TO:

54 INT. COURTHOUSE CORRIDOR - DAY   54

Larry and Althea sit on a bench, waiting nervously. He chews
his fingernails.

Down the hall, Leis, Keating, and their people stand in a
circle, laughing.

Larry is scared.

                    ALTHEA
          It's like waitin' on death row.

                    LARRY
          I might not get out of jail til I'm
          60. We should've fucked some more.

                    ALTHEA
                (sly)
          There's always the bathroom stall.

Larry glances up -- Ladies is on the left, Men is on the right.

                    LARRY
          Your place or mine?

Suddenly Isaacman runs over.

                    ISAACMAN
          The verdict's in.

                                        CUT TO:

55   INT. CINCINNATI COURTROOM - DAY   55

The packed room is dead silent. The JURY FOREMAN stares
emotionlessly at Larry.

                    JURY FOREMAN
          Guilty.

ANGLE - LARRY

He is stunned.

WIDE

The courtroom goes CRAZY. Applause breaks out. Larry is put
in handcuffs. Photographers' cameras FLASH. Keating smiles.

Larry SCREAMS furiously over the din.

                    LARRY
          All I do is print a magazine! ARE
          WE REALLY LIVING IN A FREE COUNTRY?!

Larry is hustled out by the bailiffs.

56   EXT. CINCINNATI COURTHOUSE - DAY   56

Althea runs emotionally down the steps, trying to escape. But
a throng of REPORTERS chases after her.

                    REPORTERS (adlibbed)
          Were you surprised by the verdict?
          What will you do without Larry? Are
          you ashamed to have your husband
          locked up?

Althea can't take it. She suddenly stops -- and stoically
faces them, head-on.

                    ALTHEA
          Look, I would never be ashamed of
          Larry.
                    (beat)
          Of course I wish he wasn't goin' to
          jail... But I'd rather have a man
          who stands up for what he believes
          in.

                                             CUT TO:

57   EXT. DUSTY ROAD - DAY   57

     A Lincoln Continental drives down a rural road. Althea is at
     the wheel. Ma Flynt sits next to her.

     They round a turn -- and pull up to a looming PENITENTIARY.

58   INT. PRISON - DAY   58

     Althea and Ma Flynt somberly march along with a GUARD. Ma
     carries a pie in her hands. She is on the verge of crying.

                    ALTHEA
          Try to be cheery. Larry needs all
          the strength he can get.

59   VISITING AREA   59

     Althea and Ma wait in wooden chairs. Suddenly, behind a WALL
     OF GLASS, a door flies open. Larry bounds in, wearing a prison
     jumpsuit, grinning his head off!

                    LARRY
          Hey baby, how ya shakin'?!!!
                    (beaming)
          Ma! You look great!!!

                    MA FLYNT
                    (confused)
          Larry...?

                    LARRY
          Have you heard the sales figures?!?
          We sold half a million copies
          yesterday!!

                    ALTHEA
          How do you know? --

                              LARRY
              I been on the telephone all morning!
              Newsdealers are going crazy! They
              say people can't wait to get their
              hands on what's obscene!

Ma and Althea glance strangely at each other.

                              MA FLYNT
              But Son... aren't you sad to be in
              jail?

                              LARRY
                        (ecstatic)
              I was -- til I learned acquittals
              don't sell magazines. CONVICTIONS
              do!

                              ALTHEA
              But Larry... you're lookin' at
              twenty-five years. You won't get
              outta jail until the next century.

                              LARRY
              Nope, I'm gettin' out on Monday.
              Isaacman says no appellate court will
              uphold the conviction. It's too
              screwy. So baby, smile! Hustler is
              unstoppable!!!

                                        CUT TO:

60   INT. CINCINNATI ARENA - NIGHT   60

A red, white, and blue RALLY is in progress. Supporters
whistle and cheer. Bright banners say "AMERICANS FOR A FREE
PRESS." Workers at tables register people. Girls wearing
American flags pass out buttons and bumper stickers with the
slogan, "WARNING: A CINCINNATI JURY HAS DETERMINED THAT READING
HUSTLER IS DANGEROUS TO YOUR HEALTH."

Large reproductions of recent, angry political cartoons adorn
the walls. One from Oliphant depicts a man from Cincinnati
chopping up a library's Literature section with an axe. Conrad
has one showing Lady Justice in a jail cell, weeping. Above
her, it says "HUSTLED."

BACKSTAGE

Larry is chowing down at a fancy buffet. Isaacman brings over
black political comedian DICK GREGORY.

                              ISAACMAN
              Larry, I've got somebody you should
              meet -- Dick Gregory.

                    DICK GREGORY
              (enthusiastically shaking hands)
         Man, it's a pleasure to meet you!
         We need more agitators shaking up the
         power elite.

                    LARRY
              (impressed)
         Hey, I know you... I saw you on the
         Mike Douglas Show!

                    DICK GREGORY
         Eh, that was a long time ago. They
         won't book me since I made Nixon's
         Enemies List.

LATER

An ANNOUNCER blares over the P.A.

                    BOOMING ANNOUNCER
         And now... Americans For A Free Press
         is extremely pleased to welcome to
         Cincinnati, dissident publisher and
         freedom fighter Larry C. Flynt!!

The crowd WHOOPS and CHEERS!

Larry and Jimmy peek around the curtain. Jimmy's overwhelmed.

                    JIMMY
         Wow! It was really nice of Americans
         For A Free Press to invite us here
         tonight.

                    LARRY
              (startled)
         You dummy -- that group is ME. I'm
         the one paying for all this!

OUT FRONT

Larry marches out centerstage, stopping in front of a SCREEN.
Beaming, flushed with pride, he waits for the CLAPPING to die
down... then speaks, with a building Baptist fervor:

                    LARRY
         Thank you. Let me ask you a
         question: What is more obscene?
         This...

A PICTURE of a beautiful naked woman appears on the screen, her
crotch projected over Larry's face.

                    LARRY
         Or this?

Now we SEE a horrifying crime picture: A frighteningly
mutilated body of a murder victim. The crowd is hushed.

                    LARRY
        This...?
                (another NAKED LADY)
        Or this?!
                (a DEAD SOLDIER)
        Somethin's WRONG! Sex is legal, and
        you can't show pictures of it. But
        murder is illegal, and you can show
        pictures of it!!

A MONTAGE builds. Beauty pageant contestants parade on-screen.

                    LARRY
        Look at 'em. Ain't they beautiful?
                (then NAZIS GOOSESTEP)
        But how 'bout these guys?! Grown men
        acting like sheep in a herd!
                (beat)
        If you got blood and guts, they'll
        splash you on the newspapers,
        magazines and TV! But if you got a
        pretty lady, they throw you behind
        bars! You tell me: WHAT'S MORE
        OBSCENE?

CLOSEUP - LARRY

He turns to the screen -- then suddenly stops his bombast.
Something catches in his throat, and the emotions register for
real. Larry's voice drops to a whisper.

                    LARRY
        You don't have to read Hustler to
        join our cause. This is not a pep
        rally for pornography. My conviction
        is simply a reminder that what we
        fought for 200 years ago can't be
        taken for granted!

                                        CUT TO:

61 INT. BIG BOY - DAY   61

Larry and his staffers sit around a big table, eating
sandwiches. Dick Gregory is also there, with a pile of
mimeographed Left Wing publications. Larry is ranting.

                    LARRY
        What this trial made me realize is
        that everything is political. You
        wouldn't believe the shit that's
        goin' on around us! And we've got
        a forum -- an opportunity to say
        whatever we want -- and people are
        gonna read it!

                    STAFFER
        But Larry, folks buy us for the pink.

                    LARRY
          And we're not gonna touch that. But
          the truth of the matter is that our
          articles are useless -- just fillin'
          up space!
                    (beat)
          See, why can't we have doggy-style
          on one page, and an article on how
          the Indian Nations got screwed out
          of their land on the other?

A MOTHER with KIDS walks by.

                    MOTHER
          I think you're disgusting.

                    LARRY
          Yeah? Thank you very much.

The woman blanches. She pulls her kids away.

The staffers laugh. Larry leans in.

                    LARRY
          See...? People are uninformed. They
          don't realize how the system is
          fuckin' with them. Cause we're the
          only independent major publication.

                    DICK GREGORY
          Every other magazine and newspaper
          is tied-in to Big Business and
          corporations. So they don't discuss
          this stuff.

                    STAFFER #2
          What stuff?

                    LARRY
                    (he pulls out a handwritten list)
          Who shot Malcolm X? Who shot JFK?
          Where's the cure for V.D.? Blow the
          lid off the KKK. Explain the
          Libertarian Party. Child Abuse.
          Nuclear Disasters. TV envangelists
          rippin' off poor folk.
                    (very cavalier)
          We pissed off the establishment with
          our pictures. Why can't we piss 'em
          off with our articles?

The group is stunned. Nobody knows what to say. Finally --

                    ARLO
          Jeez, Larry, you're a regular Thomas
          Paine.

CLOSEUP - LARRY

                    LARRY
          Who?

                                        CUT TO:

62   INT. MAGAZINE ART DEPARTMENT - DAY   62

     An ART DIRECTOR works at a drafting table, assembling a mock-up
     of a full-page ad parody. It says, "SOME THINGS GO TOGETHER:
     SMOKING AND SUICIDE." Below this is a photo of CANCEROUS,
     ROTTED LUNGS. He shows it to Larry.

                    ART DIRECTOR
          Is this what you wanted?

                    LARRY
               (happy as a clam)
          Perfect.

63   INT. LARRY'S OFFICE - DAY   63

     The door SLAMS open, and a hot-tempered AD SALES GUY bursts in.
     He furiously flings the smoking ad down at Larry.

                    AD SALES GUY
          What is this shit?! You're not gonna
          run this in the magazine!

                    LARRY
               (nonchalant)
          It's a public service announcement.

                    AD SALES GUY
          Larry, I gotta sell ad space. I
          guarantee if you run this, Kool
          Cigarettes will pull out!

                    LARRY
          So what? Let 'em go.

                    AD SALES GUY
               (terribly frustrated)
          But they're our only national
          advertiser! We need the income!

                    LARRY
          The hell we do. I'm gonna make 20
          million dollars this year. I don't
          need their blood money.

     The guy is stupefied.

                    LARRY
          Don't slam the door on your way out.

     The ad guy staggers away.

Larry starts opening mail. He rips opens a letter: Inside, cut-out magazine letters spell out "LARRY FLINT MUST DIE."

Larry shrugs. He opens a drawer, revealing dozens of threatening letters inside. He tosses the note in and shuts the drawer.

CUT TO:

64   INT. PHOTOGRAPHY STUDIO - DAY   64

A shoot is being set-up. A flamboyant EUROPEAN PHOTOGRAPHER is arranging colored lights. He smiles at Larry and Althea.

> EURO PHOTOGRAPHER
> (with HEAVY ACCENT)
> Three more minutes, I ready!

Althea glances at Larry.

> ALTHEA
> Who is this guy?

> LARRY
> I stole him from Vogue. He's costin'
> me a fortune, but the man's an
> artist.
> (beat)
> This centerfold's gonna be so hot,
> even the <u>mailman</u> will be jackin' off!

> ALTHEA
> (she grins)
> Thanks, 'hon.

A beat -- then Althea releases a strap and DROPS HER CLOTHES.

She's the model.

Althea struts naked across the room and plops down in front of the lights. The photographer adjusts his camera.

> ALTHEA
> I was thinkin' maybe I should hold
> a snake.

> EURO PHOTOGRAPHER
> No, no! A beauty like yours needs
> no props.

> ALTHEA
> Then what should I do?

> LARRY
> Hey, show Pavel the position that
> girl did to me last night.

> ALTHEA
> The redhead?

                        LARRY
        No, the blonde.

                        ALTHEA
            Oh, okay.

She begins to pose. The man excitedly CLICKS away.

                        EURO PHOTOGRAPHER
        Magnifique!

                        LARRY
        Now this is class.

AT THE DOOR

Arlo enters, upset.

                        ARLO
        Larry, I got shitty news! A Georgia
        prosecutor has arrested --

Arlo stops, and suddenly does a doubletake. He stammers.

                        ARLO
        Oh. Um, hi, Althea...

                        ALTHEA (o.s.)
        Hi!

                        ARLO
            (trying to get back on track)
        Er, the prosecutor's arrested some
        newsdealers for selling Hustler. So
        other retailers are scared -- they're
        pulling copies off the shelves.

Larry is shocked. A strange look comes over his face.

                        LARRY
        Well that ain't right...

                        ARLO
        We should probably call Isaacman.

                        LARRY
            (getting upset)
        NO! I wanna take care of this.
            (he grabs a PHONE)
        Hey, alert the Georgia media! The
        Cavalry is coming!

                                        CUT TO:

65   EXT. SKY - DAY   65

A bright PINK Commander Jet airplane soars through the sky.
"Hustler" is painted on the tail.

66   INT. HUSTLER PLANE   66

A lavish private plane, with thick carpeting and sofa seating.
A uniformed BARTENDER hands out drinks to incensed Larry and
a CIRCLE OF REPORTERS.

                    LARRY
          Good hard-workin' newsvendors are
          being threatened. Intimidated! If
          that's not censorship, I don't know
          what is.

                    REPORTER
          So Larry, what's your plan?

                    LARRY
          Stick myself in their face! If they
          wanna arrest someone, they can arrest
          the sonofabitch at the top of it all!

He leers wild-eyed -- unsettling everybody a bit.

AT THE BAR

stand Althea and Dick Gregory. She frowns.

                    ALTHEA
          I think he's crackin' up. Only a
          madman gets himself busted on
          purpose.

                    DICK GREGORY
          Nah... it's classic Yippie behavior.
          If you're willing to spend a couple
          hours in the pokey, you can
          accomplish a lot.

BACK ON THE GROUP

A reporter finds a lump under his seat cushion. He scrounges
around, lifting out a SEQUINED WHITE JUMPSUIT.

                    REPORTER
          Hey, weird. Look what I found.

                    LARRY
               (he grins)
          Oh, didn't I tell you? I bought this
          plane from Elvis!

                                        CUT TO:

67   INT. RATTY SHOP - DAY   67

We're in a store that sells magazines, paperbacks, and smokes.
It's packed with REPORTERS AND FILM CREWS ogling Larry.

Outside sits a COP CAR.

Althea quietly gives orders to husky BODYGUARDS.

> ALTHEA
> Look, he's pissin' off a lot of
> people today. So keep your eye out
> for any cranks in the crowd.

ON LARRY

He theatrically counts out money to a GRIZZLED OWNER.

> LARRY
> Eight, nine, one thousand dollars!
> I have now rented the Puff 'n' Read
> for the next twenty-four hours.

Larry slips a "Puff 'n' Read" visor on. He grins, then shakes
his fists at the cops outside.

> LARRY
> C'mon, coppers, COME AND GET ME!
> What are you afraid of??!

> REPORTER
> Hey Larry, what do they got against
> your magazine?

> LARRY
> (he skims a copy)
> Hmm. Could it be this month's
> interracial photo spread, "Butch and
> Peaches"? She's white and perky.
> He's black and hung.
> (with a twinkle in his eye)
> I guess Georgia just ain't ready for
> equality yet.

The reporters GASP.

68 OUTSIDE   68

The cops wait, fuming.

> COP
> This guy makes me sick.

69 INSIDE   69

Arlo shuffles from the crowd, wearing a funny hat. He's the
stooge.

> ARLO
> (play-acting)
> Hey Mister! Can I buy an autographed
> Hustler?

> LARRY
> Sure, sonny!

Arlo pulls out cash. Larry scribbles his signature and dramatically hands over the Hustler. As FLASHES explode, the cops suddenly burst in, ferociously pushing everyone aside.

>   COP
>   ALRIGHT! LARRY FLYNT, STEP OUT FROM
>   BEHIND THE COUNTER! YOU'RE UNDER
>   ARREST!!

Larry laughs impishly and thrusts his hands out for cuffs. More cameras FLASH.

>   CUT TO:

70   INT. GEORGIA JAIL - DAY   70

Isaacman irritably escorts Larry from a jail cell.

>   ISAACMAN
>   I wish you'd WARN me, before you pull
>   one of your stunts!

>   LARRY
>   Yeah yeah yeah. Hey, do me a favor
>   and give me a lift to the edge of
>   town. A guard gave me a tip on a hot
>   whorehouse.

Larry winks. Isaacman gives him a troubled look.

>   CUT TO:

71   INT. LARRY'S OFFICE - DAY   71

An editorial meeting is in progress. The staff gapes at a mockup of the next issue. The back cover says "HELP BRING JFK'S KILLERS TO JUSTICE. $1,000,000 REWARD!"

>   JIMMY
>   We're gonna pay a million bucks?!

>   LARRY
>   If it solves the murder, I will! The
>   government gets away with too much
>   shit. The so-called "mainstream"
>   media doesn't care.

>   ARLO
>   Let's hear it for the crazy man with
>   the big roll of cash.

Larry beams manically.

>   LARRY
>   Movin' on, we have to pick our
>   "Asshole Of The Month." Who's the
>   biggest hypocrite out there?

                    ALTHEA
          I nominate Jerry Falwell.

                    ARLO
                    (irked)
          You <u>always</u> nominate Jerry Falwell.

                    ALTHEA
          Well he's always an asshole. He
          takes money from poor people.

                    CHESTER
          Nah, we can't do him <u>every</u> month.
                    (beat)
          How 'bout Anita Bryant?

                    ARLO
          I say Gerald Ford.

                    JIMMY
          No. <u>Larry Flynt</u>.

Some strange looks. Then -- Larry smiles.

                    LARRY
          Good call, Bro! <u>Everybody</u> hates me.

The intercom BUZZES.

                    SECRETARY (v.o.)
          Larry, you got a phone call --

                    LARRY
          Take a message! I'm not here.
                    (back to the staff)
          Better yet: Make me Asshole of the
          YEAR!

                    ALTHEA
          Or Asshole of the DECADE!

The intercom BUZZES again.

                    SECRETARY (v.o.)
          Larry! She's calling from North
          Carolina. She says she's the
          <u>President's sister</u>. Ruth Carter
          something...

The group is shocked.

                    STAFFER
          Ruth Carter Stapleton?!

                    ARLO
          <u>She's a woman of God!</u>

                    JIMMY
          What does she want with YOU??

Everybody looks at Larry. He's on the spot.

An anxious silence. He glances down at the telephone.

It ominously sits there.

                    ALTHEA
          What, are you scared of a fuckin'
          phone??

ANGLE - LARRY

He frowns and PUNCHES on the speakerphone.

                    LARRY
          Hello... this is Larry Flynt.

RUTH speaks. She has a gentle, calming voice.

                    RUTH (v.o.)
          Well Praise the Lord, I found you!

                    LARRY
              (uncomfortable)
          Umm, Praise the Lord to you to. How
          can I help ya?

                    RUTH (v.o.)
          Well, we have a mutual friend, a
          producer at "60 Minutes." He found
          you to be quite dynamic, and
          suggested we get together. He
          thought you and I would hit it off.

Althea raises an eyebrow. Larry is baffled.

                    LARRY
          But you're an evangelist. I'm a smut
          peddler...

                    RUTH (v.o.)
          Larry, I don't believe in labels.
          I think you and I could teach each
          other a lot.
              (beat)
          So are you free for dinner tomorrow
          night?

                    LARRY
          Eh, eh, um... I'm probably busy...
          Really full schedule --

                    RUTH (v.o.)
              (cutting him off)
          You know what's nice about people
          like you and me, Mr. Flynt?

                    LARRY
          What?

                         RUTH (v.o.)
               We can <u>do anything we want.</u>

     Larry glances awkwardly around the room. Everybody stares.

                                              CUT TO:

72   EST. RUTH'S HOUSE - NIGHT   72

     A large, stately home.

73   INT. RUTH'S HOUSE - NIGHT   73

     Larry and Althea eat dinner with RUTH and her straight-up
     husband ROBERT. Ruth is a blonde, lilting Southerner with a
     beatific disposition, exuding warm, direct love. Dinner is a
     family style chow-down: Chicken, green beans, and potatoes.

                         LARRY
               Dandy chicken!

                         ALTHEA
               Good spices.

                         RUTH
               Thank you.
                    (beat)
               So Larry, do you go to church?

     Urgh. Silence. Larry and Althea glance nervously.

                         LARRY
               Oh. Er, um... I go for the big days.
               Y'know, Easter, Christmas...

                         RUTH
               Really? I hardly attend myself. I'm
               not a traditionalist.

     Larry thinks. Then he laughs.

                         LARRY
               Actually, I was fibbin'! I never go.

                         ALTHEA
               Not since I've known him.

                         RUTH
               That's alright. The rituals are
               unimportant. What matters is what's
               inside.
                    (she smiles)
               See, I'm not Baptist, Methodist, or
               Protestant. I'm just a Christian who
               goes straight to the teachings of
               Jesus.

                         ROBERT
               And does she <u>love</u> that man!

                    LARRY
          Are you a faith healer?

                    RUTH
          Goodness no -- I do spiritual
          healing. I don't mend bones, I mend
          troubled souls.

Larry is surprised -- and pleased.

                    LARRY
          Whew, that's a relief! I figured you
          were like those revival tent fakes
          that came around when I was a kid.
          Scarin' everybody with snakes.
          Wicked this, wicked that...

                    RUTH
          Hellfire and damnation. I remember
          a pastor who never talked about love.
          He only believed in the terrible
          things -- Catholics would burn in
          hell and black people were less than
          human.
                    (beat)
          That talk is unforgivable.

Beat.

                    LARRY
          Well how about that. We've got
          something in common.

                    RUTH
          Actually... there's something else.
          We're both trying to release people
          from sexual repression.

Larry's eyebrows raise.

                                        DISSOLVE TO:

74 LATER   74

The house is darkened. Althea is sleeping. Robert reads a
book.

But in the living room, Larry and Ruth still talk intently.

                    LARRY
          Tell me... Did Jimmy, I mean your
          brother, the President, ever see my
          publication?

                              RUTH
              I doubt it. After that Playboy
              interview, he's sorta bitter toward
              adult magazines. He confessed he had
              committed adultery in his heart, and
              then Billy Graham and Oral Roberts
              badmouthed him in public.

They both laugh. She thinks.

                              RUTH
              But I'm more ambivalent toward what
              you do. Sexuality is a God-given
              gift.

                              LARRY
              You bet it is! I wish more folks
              knew that.
                        (impressed)
              I figure people are too uptight.
              Nothing wrong with enjoying their
              bodies.

                              RUTH
              That's right! When I counsel
              Pentecostal women in bad marriages,
              I forget the Bible at first. I tell
              'em to get some make-up, hair
              conditioner and electric curlers,
              because Jesus wants you to be
              beautiful!

Larry is fascinated. Beat.

                              LARRY
              You are somethin'...

                              RUTH
              Larry, God created the Earth, and has
              a special purpose for all of us.
              Mine is to work with broken people --

                              LARRY
              Uh, "Broken people"?

                              RUTH
              Yes! Those who have problems with
              excessive escapes. You know,
              alcohol, drugs, sexual perversion...

                              LARRY
                        (getting nervous)
              Look -- Ruth -- I can see where this
              is going. But I'm not unhappy. I
              love my life...

                              RUTH
              And so does Jesus.

                    LARRY
                 (squirming)
           Nah, that's unlikely. I'm... pretty
           tarnished...

Ruth smiles angelically, comforting.

                    RUTH
           The Lord can forgive anyone.

Larry stares at her.

                                             CUT TO:

75 INT. CAR - NIGHT   75

Larry and Althea drive home. She's animated and fidgety, but
he seems deep in thought.

                    ALTHEA
           What a long night. Blah blah blah
           blah blah -- I thought we'd never
           leave!
                 (beat)
           What do ya say we pull over and screw
           on the hood of the car?

Larry quietly shakes his head.

                    LARRY
           Nah. Let's just go home.

                                             CUT TO:

76 INT. HUSTLER OFFICES - DAY   76

Larry shuffles glassy-eyed down a corridor. He sullenly looks
up and notices a framed editorial on a wall: A photo of himself
grinning, with the byline "Call Me Mr. Sleaze."

Larry frowns.

77 INT. CONFERENCE ROOM   77

A rowdy editorial meeting. Everybody is laughing. Larry
stares, unblinking.

                    STAFFER
           Can we really do a "Scratch 'n'
           Sniff" centerfold?!

                    ARLO
           Sure. It'll cost an extra eight
           cents an issue, but we should make
           it up in volume.

A nerdy CHEMIST in a white coat steps forward. He holds up a
pile of cards.

                              CHEMIST
              My laboratory has developed a variety
              of odor options for you.

                         JIMMY
              Lemme try them!

Jimmy swipes them away, SCRATCHES one and sticks his nose in
it. Suddenly, he YELPS in pain.

                         JIMMY
              ECH! What _is_ this?

                              CHEMIST
              Trout.

                         JIMMY
              Well it's AWFUL!

The group HOWLS crazily.

ANGLE - LARRY

gazes silently, glassy-eyed. He seems deeply troubled.
Finally, he whispers, unnoticed.

                         LARRY
              I have to go.

                                             CUT TO:

78   INT. LARRY'S OFFICE - DAY   78

The shades are drawn. In the dark, Larry huddles over the
phone, quivering.

                         LARRY
              Ruth, it's Larry! I need to talk.
                   (desperately insistent)
              I'm flying out west on business. Can
              you join me...?

                                             CUT TO:

79   EXT. SKY - NIGHT   79

All is quiet. The stars twinkle. Then Larry's pink jet soars
into view.

80   INT. HUSTLER JET - NIGHT   80

Larry and Ruth are alone in the cabin. He is doubled over and
crying.

                         LARRY
              I'm lost!

                         RUTH
              It's okay...

                    LARRY
          I've done such terrible things -- and
          I don't know why! I've published
          pictures of naked pregnant women.
          Naked bald women. Women being licked
          by grizzly bears. I'm goin' into
          another obscenity trial. I've
          cheated people. I haven't been
          faithful to my wife for one day.
          I've mocked our great country. I've
          broken at least seven of the Ten
          Commandments!

                    RUTH
               (comforting him)
          Jesus can forgive anybody.

                    LARRY
          Oh PLEASE! I need that forgiveness!!

Larry falls to his knees, his hands clasped in prayer.

Suddenly, his whole body starts shaking. His eyes roll back in
his head.

The ROAR of the jet grows.

Suddenly -- SHABOOM!

A BOLT of lightning hits the plane!

Everything shakes. The lights flash off.

TIGHT - LARRY

is having a convulsion. His skin is clammy. He begins TALKING
IN TONGUES.

WIDE

A blue mist rises. A HEAVENLY MURMUR builds, whispering,
humming, swirling around the plane.

Tears pour down Larry's face.

Then FLASH! TWO BEARDED MEN IN ROBES APPEAR IN FRONT OF HIM.
JESUS CHRIST and His Apostle PAUL. They smile warmly.

                    JESUS
          Hi Larry.

                    LARRY
               (overcome)
          W-who're you...??

                    JESUS
          I'm Jesus.

                    PAUL
          I'm Paul!

                    LARRY
          Master, forgive me!!!

Larry clutches at their robes. Jesus raises an eyebrow.

                    JESUS
          But Larry, you've been <u>very</u> bad.

                    PAUL
          So many sins, even <u>we</u> have trouble
          tabulating them.

                    LARRY
          Please. I'll change my ways. I'll
          do anything to prove my love.

                    PAUL
          <u>Anything</u>...??

They wait. Larry shudders painfully.

                    LARRY
          I'll even give up... what I hold
          dearest...

A VISION appears: Althea... slowly floating from view.

Paul is impressed.

                    PAUL
          That's quite a sacrifice.

                    JESUS
          Hmm... what else?

                    LARRY
                  (thinking)
          I will see myself castrated. I will
          give up my organs!

A loud POP -- and Larry is nude.

He looks down, and there is <u>nothing</u> between his legs! His
genitals have vanished.

                    JESUS
          Your gestures seem sincere.

                    MAN'S VOICE
          Damn. Check it out!

Larry turns -- and LENNY BRUCE strolls up.

                    LARRY
                  (startled)
          Lenny?! Lenny <u>Bruce</u>?!

                        LENNY BRUCE
               (gaping at Larry's non-genitalia)
          My friend, you are a Ken doll!

Jesus frowns.

                        JESUS
          Oh, it's you.

                        LARRY
                   (sensing tension)
          What, you two don't get along?

                        LENNY BRUCE
          Well, I said a lot of bad shit, man.
          Jesus wouldn't let me in.

                        LARRY
          Oh c'mon, Lord, do me a favor. Cut
          Lenny some slack.

                        JESUS
                   (thinking he's being conned)
          I dunno. Heaven's mighty crowded...

                        LARRY
                   (imploring)
          There's always room for one more!

Jesus considers this -- then reluctantly nods.

                        JESUS
          Alright. But you'll have to do
          penance for two.

Jesus holds out his arms. Lenny Bruce grins and jumps in them,
and Jesus, Paul, and Lenny fly away.

                        JESUS' RINGING VOICE
          Larry, go forth and spread the true
          message...

Suddenly the lights FLASH again.

KABOOM!

And we are back in

81   INT. REALITY   81

Larry lies on the floor of the plane, sobbing. Ruth cradles
him.

                        RUTH
          Are you okay?

                        LARRY
                   (still shivering)
          Ruth, it was so beautiful...

                              RUTH
                         (she smiles)
                    His love is.

               She holds Larry tighter.

                                        CUT TO:

82   INT. MANSION - NIGHT   82

               Althea is flabbergasted. Larry smiles beatifically.

                              ALTHEA
                    WHAT??!

                              LARRY
                    Honey, it was powerful and awesome.
                    I'm not ashamed to say that I cried
                    for God.

                              ALTHEA
                    Is this a JOKE?!??

                              LARRY
                         (enraptured)
                    I know it sounds goofy, but I've been
                    Born Again.

               Althea gazes, quite skeptical.

                              ALTHEA
                    What's the angle?

                              LARRY
                    No angle! I've been all the way to
                    the bottom, and now there's only one
                    way to go -- up! I'm goin' to be
                    hustling for the Lord.

                              ALTHEA
                         (sinister)
                    It was that Carter woman. I knew she
                    was gonna fuck with your head.

                              LARRY
                    Nope, Ruth had nothin' to do with it.
                    She was just the messenger.
                         (beaming)
                    But now I've seen the truth: I was
                    handed Hustler magazine as a means
                    to spread the Word.

                              ALTHEA
                    Yeah? Well I got news for you. The
                    Lord might have walked into your
                    life, but $20 million a year just
                    walked out.

                                        CUT TO:

83   EXT. LAKE - DAY   83

       Ruth, Robert, Larry, and a handful of CHRISTIANS in baptismal
       robes stand at the edge of the water. Larry is being baptized.

                         RUTH
              Do you accept the Lord Jesus Christ
              as your Savior, and reject Satan and
              all his works?

                         LARRY
                    (quiet)
              I do.

       Larry is dunked in the chilly water. He shivers blissfully.

84   EXT. FLYNT MANSION - DAY   84

       A massive PRESS CONFERENCE. A mob of REPORTERS crowd the
       steps, cameras rolling on Larry. Bodyguards watch, stone-
       faced. Larry stoically speaks, Ruth bravely at his side.

                         LARRY
              This is not a publicity stunt. I
              have been called by God!

       The crowd is flabbergasted. No one knows how to respond.

                         REPORTER #1
              Ruth, what are you doing with this
              guy??!

                         RUTH
                    (calm and dignified)
              I would ask you... have you met him
              personally and talked to him and
              looked into his eyes? Jesus says,
              "You shall be known by the fruit of
              the spirit." Well, I know what
              Larry's spirit is.

                         LARRY
              My mission is to get people to talk
              and think. You can't accept Christ
              until you first accept yourself.

85   INT. HUSTLER OFFICES - SAME TIME   85

       The staff is squeezed around a TINY TV. Their mouths are
       agape.

                         JIMMY
              I can't believe this is fuckin'
              happening!

                         ARLO
              It's the end of the world. Start
              building the ark.

ON THE TV

                    REPORTER (on TV)
      So are you shutting down Hustler?

                    LARRY (on TV)
      Nope! It's the beginning. Jesus had
      the New Testament -- well, Larry
      Flynt has the New Hustler!! There
      will still be a whole lotta sex, but
      no more explicit than what can be
      found in the Good Book.

ARLO

yanks a secretary.

                    ARLO
      Quick! Find me every dirty passage
      in the Bible.

86   EXT. PRESS CONFERENCE   86

                    LARRY
      Hustler will become a beacon of
      strength, fighting sexual repression.
      Before, I had the best journalistic
      talent in the country. Now, I've
      also got the Big Boy on my side.

Off alone, Althea shakes her head in bewilderment.

                              CUT TO:

87   MONTAGE -- NATIONAL TV COVERAGE   87

                WALTER CRONKITE (on TV)
      And in news that stunned the nation
      today, adult magazine publisher

                BARBARA WALTERS (on TV)
      Larry Flynt, in one of the most
      shocking conversions in modern
      history,

                JOHN CHANCELLOR (on TV)
      has become Born Again. Church
      leaders' responses range from disgust
      to disbelief.

We WIDEN. We're in...

88   INT. CHARLES KEATING'S OFFICE   88

Keating glares at his TV. A STILL of Larry's baptism appears.

                CHARLES KEATING
      Why are they puttin' this garbage on
      the TV?!

Keating's BLONDE, CHESTY SECRETARY shrugs.

> SECRETARY
> Do you want me to turn it off?

> CHARLES KEATING
> <u>No</u>! I might miss something.

89 INT. HUSTLER OFFICES - DAYS LATER   89

A sign says "HUSTLER MAGAZINE. JESUS CHRIST, PUBLISHER"

Larry is enlightening his confused workers.

> LARRY
> ...there will be no more photo
> spreads of women alone. Sex will be
> presented more natural, with a man
> in the picture. Something like a
> Genesis pictorial, with Adam and Eve
> gettin' it on in the Garden of Eden.
> (beat)
> The following month, I want pretty
> naked girls floating on big glass
> crucifixes. See if we can get Marjoe
> Gortner to shoot it.

Silence.

The group is astonished.

Finally, Jimmy pleads.

> JIMMY
> Larry, <u>please</u> don't do this! My
> share of the company is gonna be
> worth nothin'.

> LARRY
> Hogwash! I read a poll that 92
> percent of the American public
> believes in God. A lot less than
> that believe in pornography.

This sinks in. Slowly, Arlo's eyes widen.

> ARLO
> <u>Wait a second</u>. This is a big put-on!
> You're just trying to juice our
> circulation!

> LARRY
> (shocked)
> Arlo, how DARE you question my
> sincerity. I love my God.

In a corner, Dick Gregory stuffs beets, celery, and assorted
moss into a blender. He pours the green drink into a glass and
hands it to Larry.

                    DICK GREGORY
          Here's your lunch.

                    JIMMY
          What is that shit?!

                    DICK GREGORY
          Vegetable potassium tonic. Larry
          cleansed his soul. Now he has to
          cleanse his body.

Larry chugs it down. It leaves a ring of green on his face.

                    LARRY
          Delicious!

                                        CUT TO:

90   INT. ASSEMBLY OF GOD CHURCH - DAY   90

A packed CONGREGATION sings a spiritual. At the pulpit is a
jubilant CHOIR, a REVEREND, Ruth, and Larry, singin' away.

                    LARRY
               (belting the SONG)
          "Jesus is in the garden!
          Jesus is in the garden...!"

The hymn reaches a climax and ends.

Everyone sits. Ruth steps to the microphone.

                    RUTH
          And now, I would like to introduce
          a very special guest --
               (some HISSES and BOOS)
          Now now, I don't want any of that.
          You must be patient, because he's a
          baby Christian. Jesus loved sinners,
          and so can you. Our friend has a lot
          to teach us.
               (a warm smile)
          So now... I bring you Mr. Hustler
          Magazine himself... Larry Flynt!

Larry smiles anxiously. Ruth gives him a hug, then he takes
the mike. He softly speaks, quite tentative.

                    LARRY
          I want to thank you, heavenly Father,
          for coming into my life. Because I'm
          living proof that if it can happen
          to me, it can happen to anyone.

                    ANGRY VOICE
          Go back to HELL!

                    LARRY
                  (he nods)
            Yes... I know there are angry people.
            But I've promised God that I'll ask
            forgiveness from everyone. And
            that's a lot of folks -- since I was
            in the business of being offensive.

                 WOMAN'S VOICE
            Jesus loves you, Larry!

Larry is touched. Overly emotional, he starts weeping.

                    LARRY
            I'm so sorry! I was blinded by the
            lure of the almighty dollar. But it
            was wrong!
                  (sobbing)
            I owe every woman in America an
            apology!

                                        CUT TO:

91 EXT. NEWSSTAND - DAY   91

CLOSEUP on a HUSTLER COVER -- A boldface quote from Larry
Flynt: "We will no longer hang women up like pieces of meat."
The artwork shows a woman's legs going into a meat grinder.

A PUERTO RICAN NEWSDEALER pulls this magazine from a bundle.
He is appalled.

                 PUERTO RICAN NEWSDEALER
            Dios Mio...!

Trembling, the man puts the Hustlers on a rack. Then he
quickly blocks the covers with a board.

92 INT. HUSTLER OFFICES - DAY   92

Outside, ANGRY WOMEN jeer and throw things at the windows.

Inside, Althea yells at Larry. He calmly drinks juice.

                    ALTHEA
            It's making people SICK! People are
            walkin' up to newsstands and
            VOMITING!

                    LARRY
                  (quiet, sincere)
            I thought it was a means of
            atonement. I wanted to show that I
            was no longer willing to exploit the
            female body.

                    ALTHEA
            Well you failed miserably! Nobody
            wants religion in their porno!

                         LARRY
          But Ruth says the sex drive is the
          power of God.

                         ALTHEA
          Yeah?! Well then <u>Ruth</u> can buy the
          two million fuckin' magazines, 'cause
          no one else is!!

Larry shrugs. Althea struggles to show compassion.

                         ALTHEA
          Larry, <u>listen</u>. This has to stop.
          I can't even talk to you anymore...
          You're out of your mind!

                         LARRY
                    (offended)
          No I'm not. I can accomplish
          anything! GOD WORKS THROUGH ME! Do
          you see that wall? I CAN MAKE THAT
          WALL COME TUMBLING DOWN THROUGH SHEER
          WILL POWER!!!

                         ALTHEA
          <u>Do it</u>!

The phone rings. Larry snatches it.

                         LARRY
          Hello?

                                        INTERCUT:

93 INT. GEORGIA D.A.'S OFFICE   93

Isaacman sits with the amiable GEORGIA PROSECUTOR. Alan smiles
into the phone.

                         ISAACMAN (on phone)
          Larry, good news! I'm sittin' with
          the Georgia prosecutor...
                    (he winks at the guy)
          He's impressed that you found God,
          and he's willing to cut a plea
          bargain.

                         LARRY
          "Plea bargain"? Because the heavenly
          Father came into my life??

                         ISAACMAN
          That's right.

                              LARRY
                         (insulted)
              HECK NO! I personally sold Hustler
              to make a point -- and the Lord's
              sweet smile hasn't changed anything!
                         (triumphant)
              LET'S GO TO TRIAL!

Larry impulsively HANGS UP.

Isaacman's eyes pop. He turns weakly to the Prosecutor.

                              ISAACMAN
              Guess what?

                                             CUT TO:

94   EXT. GEORGIA COURTHOUSE AND SQUARE (LAWRENCEVILLE) - DAY   94

     Lawrenceville, Georgia. A quiet courthouse sits in a parched
     town square. All is still around the ancient frame buildings.

     THE SCENE INSIDE THE COURTHOUSE WILL BE INTERSPERSED WITH THE
     FOLLOWING IMAGES:

     A MAN walks down a side street, carrying a BRIEFCASE. He walks
     slowly, eyes looking left and right. He doesn't want to be
     noticed -- while noticing everything himself.

     The man enters an empty building.

     He goes up some stairs, then looks out the second-floor window.
     It faces the courthouse. He sits down on the floor and opens
     his briefcase. Inside is a dismantled rifle, a sandwich
     wrapped in a cellophane bag, and two cans of beer.

     The rifle -- now assembled -- rests on his lap. The man takes
     out the sandwich, opens a beer, and eats his lunch. From time
     to time he lifts his head to check outside.

95   INT. GEORGIA COURTROOM - DAY (TO BE INTERCUT WITH THE ABOVE)   95

     A JUDGE and a JURY of five women and one man sit attentively.

                              ISAACMAN
              Ladies and Gentlemen, this is a
              blatant case of prior restraint.
              Georgia newsdealers are afraid of
              selling something that has yet to be
              proven unlawful. It is 1978, and we
              are still censoring free thought!
                         (beat)
              Popular ideas don't need protection
              -- what needs to be protected is
              speech that makes people
              uncomfortable. Pornography,
              political criticism, radical
              thinking...
                              (more)

                              ISAACMAN (Cont'd)
                    this is what you find in Hustler.
                              (ominous)
                    If you start banning, where do you
                    stop?

                                                        CUT TO:

96   LATER   96

      Larry is on the stand, testifying to the PROSECUTOR.

                              PROSECUTOR
                    Mr. Flynt, how can you, as a good
                    Christian, defend this filth?!

      Larry thinks about this. Then he sighs sincerely.

                              LARRY
                    Look, I realize it's wrong to portray
                    women the way I have -- and this is
                    something I had to ask forgiveness
                    for when I accepted Christ in my
                    life. But... it's not illegal.
                    America's the greatest country in the
                    world because anybody can do whatever
                    they want!
                              (he takes a breath)
                    I think it's wrong to drink liquor,
                    but not illegal. I think it's wrong
                    to commit abortion, but not illegal.
                    Our right to think for ourselves
                    cannot be restricted!

      The jury is impressed.

                                                        CUT TO:

97   EXT. COURTHOUSE - DAY   97

      A flag stirs in a light breeze. Larry and Isaacman stride out,
      buoyant.

                              ISAACMAN
                    That was terrific, Larry. I think
                    the jury liked you.

      A few reporters scramble up.

                              REPORTERS (adlibbed)
                    Hey Larry, did you pray before going
                    in the courtroom? Is your wife
                    jealous of Ruth? Do you regret
                    changing Hustler?

                              LARRY
                    No comment, boys.

      Larry smiles and strolls off. Isaacman is stunned.

                         ISAACMAN
              Why I'm shocked! I've <u>never</u> seen you
              decline an interview.

                         LARRY
              You know, Alan, I guess I just don't
              need it anymore.

Suddenly -- BAM! BAM! BAM!

Three loud pops explode in the quiet.

ANGLE - ISAACMAN

He looks up and around, confused. Something strange has
happened. He glances down, then notices a growing bloodstain
on his shirt. He has been <u>shot</u>.

Disoriented, Isaacman peers back at Larry.

ANGLE - LARRY

is lying on the sidewalk, writhing in pain. His belly is
ripped open, and bright red guts pour out. Larry SCREAMS in
agony.

In the distance, the sound of a car SCREECHES away.

WIDE

PASSERSBY shriek at the sight and run over.

Larry is jerking spasmodically. He's swimming in blood.

Isaacman collapses in the gutter.

Courthouse doors slam open. COPS tear down the steps.

A SIREN punctuates the commotion. Suddenly an ambulance races
around the corner. It roars to a stop, and two YOUNG
PARAMEDICS jump out.

CLOSEUP - PARAMEDICS

They see the bloodbath, and freeze, horrified.

                                             CUT TO:

98 INT. AMBULANCE - DAY   98

It speeds through town. Larry lies in the back, skin pale,
eyes glassy, tubes going in. Blood is everywhere. He moans.

                         LARRY
              Oh God, give me something for the
              pain...

99   INT. BUTTON GWINNETT MEMORIAL HOSPITAL - DAY   99

A small, country medical center. Suddenly the doors fly open.
The frantic paramedics burst in, pushing Larry on a gurney.
He's in shock.

                    PARAMEDIC
          Out of our way! We got a man dyin'
          of gunshots!

                    NURSE #1
          My Lord...!

                    NURSE #2
          Get his shirt off!

                    PARAMEDIC
          Give us some blood!

                    PARAMEDIC #2
          Do we got a surgeon here?!

                                        CUT TO:

100   EST. ATLANTA AIRPORT - DAY   100

A plane touches down on the runway.

101   EXT. AIRPORT TERMINAL - DAY   101

Doors slide open, and Althea, Jimmy, and Arlo run out. Althea
is crying hysterically, and Jimmy holds her.

                    ALTHEA
          Oh shit!! Oh man...!!

Arlo flags a cab.

                                        CUT TO:

102   INT. HOSPITAL - DAY   102

Post-surgery. Larry is pasty and unconscious, bandages
engulfing his torso. Tubes and machines practically bury him.
He rhythmically sucks air through a respirator.

103   IN THE HALL   103

A shaken Althea speaks with a weary DOCTOR.

                    DOCTOR
          Two bullets, .44 magnum. One passed
          through his stomach. The other
          lodged near his spine. We had to
          remove his spleen and several feet
          of intestine.

                    ALTHEA
          Jesus Christ. Is he gonna live?

                    DOCTOR
                (somber)
        I don't know... It's already a
        miracle he made it through surgery.
        He needed twenty-four pints of blood.
                (beat)
        Actually, what saved his life was his
        intestine was empty. All he had
        consumed was juice. Otherwise, the
        infection would've killed him.

                    ALTHEA
        Can I see him?

The doctor grimaces. He has more bad news.

                    DOCTOR
        Yeah -- but -- there's one more thing
        you have to know...

104   INT. LARRY'S HOSPITAL ROOM - LATER   104

Larry breathes through nasal tubes. Slowly, his eyes flutter
open, and he gradually focuses on Althea, quietly sitting. In
a druggy, groggy stupor, he hoarsely speaks.

                    LARRY
        Did they catch the other driver?

                    ALTHEA
                (unsure)
        What other driver?

                    LARRY
        The guy in that Buick that ran into
        me.

                    ALTHEA
                (hesitant)
        Larry -- you weren't in a car
        accident. You were shot.

Larry winces in pain. He's confused.

                    LARRY
        I got <u>shot</u>?
                (pause)
        What about Isaacman?

                    ALTHEA
        He's gonna be fine. He wasn't hit
        as bad as you --

Larry's eyes widen.

Althea gulps. She dreads what she's about to say.

                          ALTHEA
          Larry... you're paralyzed from the
          waist down.

                          LARRY
                        (stunned)
          "Paralyzed"...?

                          ALTHEA
                   (trying not to cry)
          You're not gonna walk.

CLOSEUP - LARRY

His mind is reeling.

Overcome, he stammers.

                          LARRY
          From the waist down...?
                   (slowly, scared)
          Does that include my cock?

CLOSEUP - ALTHEA

She silently nods.

CLOSEUP - LARRY

He pales in anguish. It's all sinking in.

Althea leans forward, wraps her arms around him, and hugs Larry
tightly. They both start crying.

                                        DISSOLVE TO:

105 INT. HOSPITAL - ANOTHER DAY   105

An elevator DINGS open. Ruth steps out, holding flowers, and
pensively strides down the hall. We FOLLOW her to Larry's
room... discovering ARMED COPS standing guard.

106 INSIDE THE ROOM   106

The doctor and Althea watch typical Flyntesque commotion.
Larry's bandages have been stripped off, and Rudy the
Photographer is snapping shots of the horrific exposed wounds.
Larry's belly looks like raw hamburger.

Larry mumbles orders in a slurred speech.

                          LARRY
          Move in tighter. Good and gory. I
          want those bastards to see what they
          did to me.

                    DOCTOR
                 (irked)
          <u>Germs</u>, Mr. Flynt! Can we wrap this
          up??

                    LARRY
          Shut up, Doc. We're racin' the
          deadline for next month's issue.
                 (surly)
          But if you wanna make yourself
          useful, gimme another four milligrams
          of Morphine.

ANGLE - RUTH

She silently enters. Ruth comes over and softly kisses Larry
on the forehead.

                    RUTH
          Larry, how are you?

                    LARRY
          The pain is indescribable. I'm in
          hell...

                    RUTH
                 (she takes his hand)
          No you're not. Remember, you belong
          to God. He has not forsaken you.

                    ALTHEA
                 (muttering)
          Bullshit.

Ruth ignores this.

Larry peers at Ruth. Deeply troubled, he struggles to contain
his rage and grief.

                    LARRY
          Ruth... they should've hit me in the
          heart, because my life is over! I'm
          never gonna walk again. I'm never
          gonna have children with Althea. My
          body feels like it's on fire.

                    RUTH
          I know, honey, I know...
                 (upset, trying to be strong)
          But guard against bitterness. God
          will see you through this.

CLOSEUP - LARRY

He stares. His eyes are very sad.

>   LARRY
>   There is no God.

                                              CUT TO:

107   INT. HUSTLER MAGAZINE OFFICES - DAY   107

A cross gets taken off the wall. The staff is gathered, and
Althea addresses them.

>   ALTHEA
>   We're goin' back to the old days.
>   Crank up the sleaze, and get rid of
>   the crosses. We are Porn Again.

>   STAFFER
>   When's Larry comin' back?

>   ALTHEA
>   I dunno...
>   (trying to act strong)
>   But let's just put out a rag he'd be
>   proud of.

108   INT. PRINTING PRESSES - DAY   108

Hustlers rumble down the presses. The cover artwork is again
loud and raunchy. It screams "PORN AGAIN! ALL GODLESS ISSUE!"
Inside, the Publisher's Statement has -- Althea's picture. The
headline says "A NATION GONE GUN CRAZY"...

                                              CUT TO:

109   EXT. HOSPITAL - DAY   109

Larry finally leaves the hospital, gaunt and shivering. Althea
silently pushes him in a WHEELCHAIR. Larry's entourage and
BODYGUARDS form a cluster around him.

Larry's limo waits by the curb. The DRIVER runs over and opens
a door, and Alan Isaacman steps out, weak but healed. Isaacman
goes to Larry, and they warmly shake.

Althea then rolls Larry up to the car. An awkward pause. The
driver and a bodyguard hurry over and unsurely lift Larry from
the wheelchair. They place him into the car.

110   INT. LIMO   110

Larry sits in back with Althea, Jimmy, Arlo, and Isaacman. The
car takes off, and Larry mumbles in a slurred speech.

>   LARRY
>   What do we know?

>   ALTHEA
>   The FBI says they got no leads.

                    ARLO
          It's fuckin' fishy! A high-powered
          rifle picks off two men in broad
          daylight in front of a courthouse,
          and nobody sees anything!

                    JIMMY
                 (to Larry)
          Who do you think would wanna shoot
          you?

                    LARRY
          Just open a phone book. Who
          wouldn't?!

Everyone contemplates this.

                    ARLO
          My guess is the CIA did it. They're
          freaked about that million dollars
          you offered for JFK's killers.

                    ALTHEA
          Hey, what about that interracial
          photo spread? It could be the KKK.

                    JIMMY
          Or the Mob. They control most of the
          porn business.

                    ARLO
          Or the hard-core Religious Right.
          They control all the fanatics.

                    ISAACMAN
                 (a wry smile)
          I see. You've narrowed it down to
          every dangerous wacko in the country.

Althea shakes her head.

                    ALTHEA
          Larry, you're always gonna have to
          watch your back.

                    LARRY
                 (he woozily thinks)
          Or go someplace where perverts are
          welcome.

                                        CUT TO:

111 MONTAGE   111

It's... LOS ANGELES! We see an aerial shot of the Hollywood
sign, then other absurd images of the city.

112   EXT. BEVERLY HILLS - DAY   112

Palm trees sway against a blue sky. We're in BEVERLY HILLS,
California. Luxurious mansions glisten on wide, beautiful
streets. But there is an anomoly: A HUGE ESTATE turned into a
fortress. Behind iron gates, uniformed SOLDIERS with Uzis
patrol the grounds.

A handsome JOGGING COUPLE runs by. They look in -- and shake
their heads in dismay.

113   EXT. FLYNT'S L.A. MANSION - DAY   113

It is an insane compound. The house is an unbelievable
Spanish/Roman Xanadu extravaganza. Statuary decorates the
broad lawns. Koi swim in a lake around the courtyard.
Matching tennis courts, swimming pools, and waterfalls give a
symmetry to both sides of the spread. Armed guards walk about.

114   INT. L.A. MANSION - DAY   114

Lavish, stifling opulence. Green marble onyx floors, stained
oak walls, Venetian lamps, oil paintings, a grand piano, a
restaurant-sized kitchen, an exercise room with body-building
equipment... And no people.

115   INT. BEDROOM   115

A large canopied bed sits in an airless, dim, spooky bedroom.
Larry lies in the bed, moaning like the living dead. He's
shaking, sweating terribly, dull eyes glazed over.

Althea sits forlornly in a chair, watching. Quietly, she gets
up and tiptoes to the door, for a break. Suddenly --

                         LARRY
               Don't go.

Althea turns. Larry weakly gestures, in a woozy whisper.

                         LARRY
               Hon', it hurts so much... I need...
               a higher dose... try twelve
               milligrams...

Althea winces. She glances at Larry's nightstand.

It is literally spilling over with DRUGS. Dozens of bottles,
pills, vials...

Althea sighs. She fills a syringe, checks the needle, then
injects Larry.

He rolls over, GROANING in agony.

                         LARRY
               Ohhh, you can't imagine what it's
               like...

ANGLE - ALTHEA

No reply. Althea just stares at Larry, then at the needle in
her hand.

She thinks, then refills the syringe and rolls up her own
sleeve. Althea injects herself. As the drug consumes her
body, she starts shivering uncontrollably. Althea climbs into
bed and lies down next to Larry...

A pause, then she reaches over and hits a BUTTON.

OUTSIDE THE BEDROOM

A hulking 500-pound STEEL DOOR swings shut and locks with a
thud.

Beat. A SUPER appears: "1979"

Then another: "1980"

Then another: "1981"

Then another: "1982"

Then another: "1983"

The vault door is still closed.

116   INT. BEDROOM   116

The room has become a chamber of horrors: Dirty, dark, and
clammy. Years of insane drug use have aged Althea and Larry
beyond belief: Larry looks wasted and has put on a bloated
fifty pounds. Althea is gaunt, haggard, and a punked-out
junkie. She wears a nose ring, and track marks run up and down
her arms.

They converse in an incoherent, narcotic fog.

                    ALTHEA
          I've got a fuckin' headache that
          won't stop.

                    LARRY
          Clean my bedsores.

                    ALTHEA
          Just wait til after breakfast.

She stumbles over to a dressing area. The room is a warehouse
of drug paraphernalia: Bottles, pills, booze, dirty needles,
rubber tubes, scattered all over the counters and floor...

Althea takes a bartender's jigger and scoops up a mountain of
powder. She dumps it into a martini shaker, grinds in some
pills, then pours in half a bottle of gin. She shakes the
cocktail. Larry groggily licks his lips.

Althea pours the concoction into two dirty glasses, then staggers back over.

                    LARRY
          Here's to us.

They share zombied smiles, then CLINK glasses.

They drink. Suddenly the INTERCOM buzzes. Larry garbles into it.

                    LARRY
          Mrmyeah?

                    VOICE (on intercom)
          Larry, it's Dr. Bob.

Larry hits a BUTTON. Suddenly the steel door's giant lock WHIRS and unclicks. It starts opening...

And in walks DOCTOR BOB, a groovy Beverly Hills internist. He enters, fake-cheery, swinging a Gucci bag.

                    DR. BOB
          So how's my favorite patient?

                    LARRY
               (slurry)
          Lousy. It feels like I'm standin'
          in boiling water while a claw hammer
          rips the meat off my bones.

                    DR. BOB
          Ah. So no change.

Althea sloppily unlocks a safe by the bed. She removes a HUGE WAD OF MONEY.

                    ALTHEA
          Enough with the chit-chat. What do
          you got for us today?

                    DR. BOB
          Well, y'know, Althea, it's getting
          difficult. The hospital pharmacist
          keeps asking questions --

                    ALTHEA
               (rudely throwing money at him)
          Here's twelve or fifteen grand.

The good Doc shrugs.

                    DR. BOB
          But you're such a sweetheart, how can
          I let you down?

He gathers up the money, then snaps open his Gucci bag. The Doctor starts lifting out pill bottles and pharmaceutical jars.

Larry groans unhappily. He tries to focus enough to talk serious.

> LARRY
> Doctor... I've been thinkin'. I wanna have them cut my spinal cord.

> ALTHEA
> (surprised)
> Larry...?!

> LARRY
> I don't care if I lose control of my body -- I can't take the pain anymore!

Dr. Bob nods grimly. While Althea rummages through the drugs, he sits down with Larry.

> DR. BOB
> Larry, we might have a better option. I just heard about a new experimental laser surgery at Duke University. They cauterize the sensory nerves on the spinal cord, so you stop feeling the pain.

> LARRY
> (intrigued, but dubious)
> What are the side effects?

> DR. BOB
> There aren't supposed to be any.

Larry's eyes widen.

                                        CUT TO:

117   INT. DUKE UNIVERSITY MEDICAL CENTER - DAY   117

Surgery. Larry lies unconscious on his stomach, while a burning LASER cuts into his spine.

                                        DISSOLVE TO:

118   INT. MEDICAL CENTER - DAYS LATER   118

Althea walks shakily down a corridor, carrying flowers. She looks hellish.

Althea enters Larry's room -- and he's propped up in bed, alert and ferociously energetic. He eats jello with a wild hunger.

> ALTHEA
> Hey, how are ya doin'?

> LARRY
> Real good!

                          ALTHEA
          No... seriously...

                          LARRY
          I mean it, I'm hunky-dory!
                    (he frantically shovels the jello
                    into his mouth)
          It's unbelievable! I feel like I can
          fly!! For the first time since those
          fuckin' bullets, I don't hurt!

She smiles weakly and hugs him.

                          ALTHEA
          That's cool. We should celebrate and
          party.

Althea whips out a BAG OF COLORED PILLS.

Larry stops eating. He gives her a strange look.

                          LARRY
          No, don't you understand? I don't
          need that stuff anymore.

                          ALTHEA
                    (she picks out some red ones)
          Okay. Then just a couple uppers --

                          LARRY
                    (determined)
          NO, I don't want any of that shit!
          I want my mind back. I'm stoppin'
          cold turkey.

CLOSEUP - ALTHEA

She is hurt, angry, and confused.

                          ALTHEA
          Oh, uh... terrific. Then what the
          fuck am I supposed to do??!

                                              CUT TO:

119   EST. NEW HUSTLER L.A. OFFICES - DAY   119

A beautiful Beverly Hills building gleams.

120   INT. HUSTLER'S L.A. OFFICES - DAY   120

Hustler has relocated to swanky offices: Lavish headquarters
filled with expensive antiques and fine art. Suited employees
carry on a low hum of activity.

Suddenly the front lobby elevator DINGS -- and Larry comes
barreling out, speeding in a GOLD-PLATED WHEELCHAIR. He shouts
out.

                    LARRY
          THE PERVERT IS BACK!

121 INT. CONFERENCE ROOM - DAY   121

     Larry sits at the head of a long table, addressing the troops.
     All the familiar staffers, plus NEW CORPORATE FACES, listen.
     Embossed on the wall are gold letters, "LFP."

                    LARRY
          Circulation is down by a third. The
          articles suck. The color
          reproduction is terrible, and the
          women look like three-dollar whores.
                    (repulsed)
          It's just like every other skin mag
          on the rack.

     A good-looking BLOW-DRIED JERK stands up.

                    BLOW-DRIED JERK
          Mr. Flynt, I don't want to step on
          your toes, but things have changed
          since you were actively running the
          company.
                    (patronizing)
          I mean, I look back at that stuff you
          did in the '70s, and... it's sort of
          racy, and crazy... but the country is
          different now. Reagan has rebuilt
          America, and there's a sense of hope --

                    LARRY
          You're fired.

                    BLOW-DRIED JERK
                    (taken aback)
          Excuse me?

                    LARRY
          Get the fuck out of my building.
          Hans, escort him out. Throw him down
          the garbage chute. Just get out of
          my face.

     A GERMAN BODYGUARD picks up the jerk. Jimmy jumps up.

                    JIMMY
          But Larry! He's V.P. of marketing.

                    LARRY
                    (enraged)
          You questionin' my authority, Jimbo?!
                    (he points at "LFP" on the wall)
          You see that?? It stands for "Larry
          Flynt Publications"! That makes me
          king! So who else has a problem???

     The group is stupefied.

Nobody speaks. Jimmy scrunches down in his seat.

Finally, Arlo breaks the mood --

> ARLO
> So Larry, what's the plan?

CLOSEUP - LARRY

His face hardens.

> LARRY
> The plan... is to CREATE CHAOS. This
> magazine will be a tool to bring
> America to its knees -- and make 'em
> suck my dead dick!!
> (bellowing)
> Cause they're askin' for it! I was
> shot going into a courthouse, and
> nobody was arrested! Nobody was
> investigated! The government just
> looked the other fuckin' way!!!

Larry is shaking. He catches his breath.

> LARRY
> They stripped me of my manhood. I
> have only half a life left... the
> half with a brain. Well, I'm gonna
> use it to get back at the people who
> did this to me. SO WATCH OUT! I'm
> an anarchist with a hundred million
> dollars to shove up their collective
> ass.

> CUT TO:

122   INT. FLYNT MANSION - NIGHT   122

Larry sits in his wheelchair, silently staring.

On the couch, Althea is fucking another WOMAN. Althea throws
her head back, enjoying the domination. A pause, then she
glances over at Larry.

> ALTHEA
> Is it good, baby? Can you see
> everything, baby?

Larry nods. Suddenly, the woman starts GROANING with pleasure.
Her moans get louder, more intense.

Larry snaps from his reverie. Slowly realizing his isolation,
he glumly zooms away in his wheelchair.

ACROSS THE ROOM

Larry stops at the big screen TV. He morosely clicks it on.

On the TV, JERRY FALWELL appears, booming in front of American flags and a giant choir.

> JERRY FALWELL (on TV)
> Get them saved, baptized, and
> registered!
>> (he holds up a BIBLE)
> If a man stands by this Book, vote
> for him. If he doesn't, <u>don't</u>!

Larry frowns. He CHANGES the channel --

"DYNASTY" appears. JOAN COLLINS takes a bath.

Another channel CHANGE --

An urgent NEWS REPORTER delivers a live report.

> REPORTER (on TV)
> ...received word that U.S. troops
> have just invaded the Caribbean
> island of Grenada. Details are
> sketchy, due to a press blackout...

ANGLE - LARRY

What?! He is shocked, outraged, thinking, scheming...

> LARRY
> That takes fuckin' nerve...!

> CUT TO:

123   EXT. LINCOLN MEMORIAL - DAY   123

A crowded PRESS CONFERENCE. Larry reads gravely from a statement, with Isaacman standing deadpan at his side.

> LARRY
> Today I filed suit in U.S. District
> Court against Secretary of State
> George Shultz and Secretary of
> Defense Caspar Weinberger. This
> press ban in Grenada is a national
> disgrace! There is no justification
> in locking reporters out -- it's a
> violation of constitutionally
> protected First Amendment rights.

All the REPORTERS shout out questions.

> PATRONIZING TV REPORTER
> What on earth does this have to do
> with Hustler?

                    LARRY
                 (eyes burning)
          It has NOTHING to do with Hustler,
          you jerkoff! I put out a monthly
          with a three-month leadtime! I'm
          doin' this for you, because you
          pussies at CBS and ABC and NBC are
          too chickenshit to fight for the
          public's right to know!!

The crowd is shocked silent.

Larry rages.

                    LARRY
          Hundreds of Americans have been
          slaughtered, and the mad bomber
          Reagan hides behind presidential
          privilege and national security!
          What is going on? You sure can't
          tell from reading a White House press
          release!

                                            CUT TO:

124   EST. CAPITOL BUILDING - DAY   124

125   INT. CONGRESSIONAL MAILROOM - DAY   125

A MAILCLERK nonchalantly rolls a cart down a corridor, sticking
Hustlers into every official Congressional mailbox. On the
COVER, a naked girl pulls down Uncle Sam's pants.

We see a few names on the mailboxes: Jesse Helms, Jack Kemp,
Barney Frank, Geraldine Ferraro, Strom Thurmond...

126   EST. SUPREME COURT BUILDING - DAY   126

127   INT. SUPREME COURT MAILROOM - DAY   127

Another MAILCLERK delivers Hustlers to the Justices' mailboxes:
Honorable William H. Rehnquist, Honorable Sandra Day
O'Connor...

We HEAR Larry dictating a letter.

                    LARRY (v.o.)
          "Dear Esteemed Public Servant...
          because you need to stay informed on
          all social issues, I have taken the
          liberty of gifting you a
          complimentary subscription to
          Hustler, our country's greatest porn
          magazine."

                                            CUT TO:

128   INT. HOUSE OF REPRESENTATIVES - DAY   128

        Completely unhinged HOUSE REPS bicker on the floor. A few wave
        their complimentary Hustlers.

                            HOUSE REP #1
                    I am repulsed! We are the victims
                    of a sick publicity stunt!

                            HOUSE REP #2
                    It's outrageous! I call on all
                    decent members of Congress to remove
                    themselves from this smut mailing
                    list.

                                                        CUT TO:

129   INT. HUSTLER OFFICES - DAY   129

        Larry LAUGHS naughtily at Dick Gregory.

                            LARRY
                    Now they're petitionin' the
                    Postmaster General to stop the
                    magazines! These guys are trippin'
                    over themselves -- nobody wants to
                    be the last one on the Hill
                    subscribing to Hustler!

                            DICK GREGORY
                    Keep it coming. Don't let 'em off
                    easy.

                            LARRY
                    Hell NO! I'm gonna drag 'em into
                    Federal court and make 'em read the
                    thing. I've got a constitutional
                    right to communicate with my elected
                    representatives!

        Dick shakes his head, impressed.

                            DICK GREGORY
                    Where does a guy without an education
                    get ideas like this?

        Larry giggles and coyly picks up a NEWSPAPER.

                            LARRY
                    I just read the newspaper!
                            (he scans the front page)
                    Why, look at all these interesting
                    stories: Korean jetliner 007 shot
                    down over Russia. Moral Majority
                    backs Reagan for reelection. Alfred
                    Bloomingdale's mistress found
                    murdered. John DeLorean busted in
                    FBI cocaine sting.
                            (more)

                              LARRY (Cont'd)
                          (beat; he grins)
                    See, I just say to myself: How can
                    these things affect Larry Flynt?

                                                        CUT TO:

130   INT. NICE BEDROOM - NIGHT   130

      The CBS Newsman and his WIFE are asleep in bed.

      Suddenly the phone RINGS, jolting them awake. The guy looks at
      the clock -- 2:48 a.m. -- then groggily answers the phone.

                          CBS NEWSMAN
                    H-hello...?

                          LARRY (v.o.)
                          (cheery, loud)
                    Hey! Guess who?!

                          CBS NEWSMAN
                    Hrmm...?

                          LARRY (v.o.)
                    It's your old pal Larry Flynt! We
                    met on "60 Minutes"!
                          (beat)
                    Well anyway, you sound busy, so I'll
                    cut to the chase. Are you interested
                    in seeing videotape of the FBI
                    selling John DeLorean 50 kilos of
                    cocaine?

      The guy's eyes bulge.

131   EXT. FLYNT MANSION - LATE THAT NIGHT   131

      A Cadillac roars up. The CBS Newsman jumps out, a coat over
      his pajamas. He runs to the front door and RINGS the bell.

      A pause -- then zombie Althea whips open the door, spiked hair
      popping. The reporter jumps, startled.

132   INT. FLYNT MANSION - MINUTES LATER   132

      The CBS Newsman sits in Larry's room, slobbering with
      excitement. Larry fiddles with the video equipment.

                          ALTHEA
                    Can I get you a beer... salad...
                    Pringles...?

                          CBS NEWSMAN
                    No -- nothing. Can I just see the
                    tape?

      Larry cockily fingers the VCR... then hits PLAY.

ANGLE - THE THREE TVS

Grainy black-and-white surveillance video comes on. JOHN
DELOREAN and UNDERCOVER FEDERAL AGENTS sit around a tacky hotel
room. An agent lifts a suitcase onto a table.

ANGLE - LARRY AND THE NEWSMAN

                    LARRY
          See, that's the undercover agent,
          selling the coke to DeLorean. He
          needs the money to save his car
          company --

                    CBS NEWSMAN
          Shh!

ANGLE - THE TV

The agent opens the suitcase -- revealing it's full of BAGS OF
COCAINE. DeLorean grins and fondles the packets.

                    LARRY
          Look how happy he is! That coke's
          worth five million dollars! Hey --
          now DeLorean's toastin' them with
          champagne!

Suddenly another MAN enters the scene.

                    LARRY
          Uh-oh. It's the FBI! Sorry John,
          you're BUSTED!
               (he cackles)
          He don't know what hit him!

The agent HANDCUFFS DeLorean.

BACK ON THE CBS NEWSMAN

His jaw is wide open.

                    CBS NEWSMAN
          Jesus Christ. How the hell did you
          get this??!

                    LARRY
          Oh, friends in high places.
               (coy)
          So is CBS interested?

                                        CUT TO:

133   INT. U.S. DISTRICT COURT - DAY   133

The courtroom of calm, controlled JUDGE THOMAS MANTKE. Over
time, this poor man is going to be driven crazy by Larry.

Three GROUPS OF LAWYERS shout over each other.

                    FEDERAL ATTORNEY
          CBS cannot be allowed to air the
          tape! It's stolen government
          evidence!

                    CBS ATTORNEY
          The tape is genuine and newsworthy.
          We have a right to broadcast it!

                    DELOREAN ATTORNEY
          This leak will make a fair trial
          IMPOSSIBLE! My client Mr. DeLorean
          will never find an impartial jury!

     Mantke rubs his head.

                                             CUT TO:

134 CLOSEUP - TELEVISION   134

     The "60 MINUTES" stopwatch logo TICKS away.

     The fuzzy DeLorean VIDEO comes on.

                    DELOREAN (on TV)
          It's better than gold!

                                             CUT TO:

135 INT. HUSTLER OFFICES - DAY   135

     Larry and the staff flip CHANNELS on a TV.

                    NEWSCASTER (on TV)
          Today the John DeLorean trial was
          postponed indefinitely --

     Another channel.

                    NEWSCASTER #2 (on TV)
          DeLorean attorneys plan to ask for
          a dismissal of all charges --

     The group is flabbergasted.

                    ARLO
          This is fuckin' unbelievable!

                    ALTHEA
               (strung out, head bobbing)
          I don't understand... what do you
          have to do with DeLorean...?

                    LARRY
          Nothing.

                         ARLO
               Well, Mr. Flynt, this is certainly
               Grade A Anarchy. I don't know how
               you're gonna top this.

Larry wiggles his eyebrows...

                                        CUT TO:

136   EXT. COLUMBUS HUSTLER BAR - DAY   136

Larry is in front of his old Hustler bar. He is dressed-up,
and his gold-plated wheelchair is now decorated with a little
string of American flags.

Larry booms out to a row of CAMERAMEN.

                         LARRY
               I hearby announce my candidacy for
               the Presidency of these United States
               of America!

The crowd GASPS. Tons of FLASHBULBS go off.

                         LARRY
               I am running as a Republican rather
               than as a Democrat because I am
               wealthy, white, pornographic and,
               like the nuclear-mad cowboy Ronnie
               Reagan, I have been shot for what I
               believe in. My platform is simple:
               Free thought, individual liberties,
               and civil rights for all mankind.
               Big Brother Government and the Moral
               Majority should stay out of our
               lives! When elected, my primary goal
               will be to eliminate sexual ignorance
               and venereal disease.

                                        CUT TO:

137   EXT. WHITE HOUSE - DAY   137

Larry speaks in front of the White House. He's wearing a
"Larry Flynt for President" T-shirt. Althea stands
uncomfortably next to him, in black leather and green hair.
HOMELESS PEOPLE watch.

                         LARRY
               As President, I will immediately
               initiate massive social reforms:
               Fines will be levied against all
               Americans who fail to vote. Teachers
               will earn at least $30,000 per year.
               And I will ensure that the ERA is
               ratified.
                         (more)

LARRY (Cont'd)
    (beat)
Think about it: Who would you prefer
as your President -- an addle-brained
Hollywood ham, or a smut peddler who
cares?

                                        CUT TO:

138   INT. BOWLING ALLEY - NIGHT   138

Under a banner that says "PAINT THE WHITE HOUSE PINK," Larry
sits in his wheelchair in the center lane. The BOWLERS listen
to him over a P.A. system.

                    LARRY
What qualifications are we looking
for in our next President? First of
all, he should be a good con man, so
he can persuade blue-collar America
that forty-hour weeks on an assembly
line is all you can expect from life.
He should've been raised in poverty
eating grits and red-eye gravy, so
he knows how important a steak is to
us working people. And he should
have paid for the services of at
least one prostitute, so that he
knows what it's like to be
face-to-face with Yasir Arafat.

Hmm. The bowlers scratch their heads.

Larry rebounds.

                    LARRY
You folk deserve more than a trickle-
down. So vote for me next November!

The crowd CHEERS and WHISTLES enthusiastically.

139   INT. KEATING'S LINCOLN SAVINGS OFFICE - DAY   139

Charles Keating is busy in his new, obsessively clean office.
A glass Madonna sits on his desk.

Suddenly the phone RINGS. He grabs it.

                 CHARLES KEATING
Charlie Keating here.
    (beat, he pales in horror)
Who's running for President??!

                                    WIPE TO:

140   INT. HUSTLER OFFICES - DAY   140

Larry, Arlo, and hazy Althea review magazine artwork.

                              ARLO
                    ...and here's next month's inside
                    front cover. A parody of a Campari
                    Liquor Ad -- Jerry Falwell describes
                    his "first time."

They examine the ad. Falwell's face beams out.

                              ALTHEA
                    Cool -- I hate that guy.

                              ARLO
                    Yeah. Callin' himself the "Moral
                    Majority"... implies the rest of us
                    are an <u>immoral minority</u>.

                              LARRY
                    It's fascism.
                              (beat)
                    Tell ya what: Instead of screwing a
                    hooker, why don't we have Falwell
                    makin' it with his own <u>mama</u>?

                              ARLO
                              (he LAUGHS)
                    El Jefe, you're the best.

A staffer walks toward them, reading a newspaper. Larry
squints... and we see a headline with the word "DeLOREAN"...

Larry starts scowling...

The guy is upon them... Larry suddenly blows a gasket and
angrily SNATCHES the paper.

                              LARRY
                    HEY! What's the big idea, restartin'
                    the DeLorean trial?!

                                                  CUT TO:

141   INT. ISAACMAN'S LAWFIRM - DAY   141

Larry shouts at Isaacman.

                              LARRY
                    For all the money I pay your fancy
                    pants lawfirm, you'd think you could
                    help me out!!!

                              ISAACMAN
                              (bewildered)
                    With <u>what</u>? You have nothing to do
                    with <u>this</u> trial! It's none of your
                    BUSINESS!!

                         LARRY
             Yeah -- but it's my hobby.
                    (he shrugs)
             Now what if I had another tape? And
             this one was <u>so inflammatory</u>, it
             could bring down the entire fuckin'
             federal government?!?

Isaacman stares tiredly.

                         ISAACMAN
             Do you have this tape...?

                         LARRY
                    (perky)
             I will.

                                        CUT TO:

142   EXT. FLYNT MANSION - DAY   142

A crazed press conference. The lawn is filled with news vans.
Swarming REPORTERS jostle to hear Larry, proudly centerstage.
Security guards with automatic weapons patrol the courtyard.

                         LARRY
             Ladies and Gentlemen of the press,
             when I released the John DeLorean
             videotape, it may have given the
             impression that he was guilty.
                    (beat)
             So, today I have an audiotape
             <u>absolutely proving</u> that DeLorean was
             threatened by the government and
             coerced into this drug deal!

The crowd goes NUTS.

                         REPORTER #1
             Where'd you get the tape?!

                         LARRY
             None of your business. I can't
             reveal my source. Now quiet please!

The group obediently HUSHES.

Larry holds up the tiny Sony recorder. Biting his lip, he
presses "Play."

INAUDIBLE VOICES come out of the horribly overamplified little
machine. Two men's distorted voices MUMBLING.

The crowd strains to understand. People scrunch up their
faces, trying to make out a word here or there.

                         ARLO
             If anyone needs it, I've got the
             official transcript right here.

Arlo waves a pile of PAPERS. Reporters mob him, snatching them
from his hands.

ANGLE - TWO REPORTERS

examine the TRANSCRIPT. It is a scrawled hand-written Xerox.
The completely UNINTELLIGIBLE TAPE keeps playing in the b.g.

                    REPORTER #2
          I can't understand anything. What's
          it say?

                    REPORTER #1
                 (reading the transcript)
          DeLorean: "I've pulled out. I don't
           want any part of narcotics. All I
           wanted was an investment to save the
           company."
          Fed: "John, you honor your part of the
           deal. That way you live longer."
          DeLorean: "Please! I just want out."
          Fed: "How is your little daughter?
           Wanna get her head smashed?"

                    REPORTER #2
          Jesus Christ!

DOWN FRONT

The murky TAPED VOICES stop. The crowd is in a state of shock.

                    LARRY
          Really something, ain't it?! It's
          amazing what our government gets away
          with.

People shake their heads, astonished.

                    REPORTER
          Can we hear the tape again?

                    LARRY
          Sure.

Larry reaches for the tiny recorder and presses the button.

But nothing happens.

Larry examines the machine, then suddenly gets bizarrely upset.
He angrily waves the recorder in the air.

                    LARRY
          Alright, <u>who stole the tape</u>?!

WIDE

Total confusion.

Nobody understands what's happening.

                          LARRY
              SHUT THE GATES! Nobody's gettin' off
              this property!!

Big iron gates start closing.

Utter pandemonium.

Reporters are trampling each other.

TIGHT - ARLO AND LARRY

Larry is pleased. Then Arlo tiredly leans in.

                          ARLO
              Enough already. Let 'em go.

                                                  CUT TO:

143   INT. JUDGE MANTKE'S CHAMBERS - DAY   143

Federal Judge Mantke stares incredulously at the morning
newspaper. The headline screams, "FLYNT TAPE REVEALS FBI
ENTRAPPED DELOREAN."

Mantke fumes.

                          MANTKE
              I cannot believe this! Issue a
              subpoena to Mr. Flynt. I want this
              tape on my desk 9 a.m. tomorrow.

                                                  WIPE TO:

144   INT. MANSION - DAY   144

Larry shouts into a phone.

                          LARRY
              You tell that judge I wiped my ass
              with his subpoena.
                    (beat)
              And if anyone tries comin' after me,
              I'll shoot 'em between the eyes!

                                                  WIPE TO:

145   INT. MANTKE'S COURTROOM - DAY   145

Mantke holds another newspaper: "FLYNT DEFIES UNITED STATES."
The judge is perplexed.

                          MANTKE
              Why is your client doing this?!

                          ISAACMAN
                    (uncomfortable)
              My client is a very complicated man.
              I believe he's manic-depressive.

Mantke burns. He scribbles his signature on a form.

                    MANTKE
          Well I'll give him something to be
          depressed about. I'm issuing a bench
          warrant for his arrest.

                                        WIPE TO:

146 EXT. FLYNT COMPOUND - DAY   146

HELICOPTERS buzz Larry's house. Rain pours.

A motorcade of Federal MARSHALS storm the premises. They bust
in the gate, jump from vehicles and serpentine up to the house.

Startled Flynt security guards run out, defiantly pointing
machine guns.

                    GUARD
          Freeze!

                    MARSHAL
               (unamused)
          Drop that toy, or I'll kick your ass.
          We're federal marshals.

On the muddy street, NEWS VANS with satellite dishes screech
up.

147 INT. HOUSE   147

Marshals leap the stairs, three at a time. Chinese vases CRASH
in their wake.

The butler runs scared.

But a marshal grabs him by the neck.

                    MARSHAL
          Where is he?

                    BUTLER
               (shaking)
          In there.

WIDE

The butler points at the STEEL DOOR. The marshal is
flabbergasted. He tugs at it.

                    MARSHAL
          What the hell?

A sudden SQUAWK from the intercom.

                    LARRY (over intercom)
          You'll never get me! I'm behind 500
          pounds of reinforced steel!

148   INSIDE THE BEDROOM   148

Larry is watching a bank of TVs. Althea is sprawled woozily on
the bed, eating Captain Crunch. On TWO TVs is live news
coverage outside the house: Helicopters zoom through frame.
On the THIRD TV is "The Joker's Wild."

                    LARRY
          I've got ABC and NBC, but CBS is
          still runnin' some game show.
                    (disenchanted)
          Man, what kind of fucked-up
          priorities do they have...?

Suddenly "SPECIAL BULLETIN" appears. Larry is instantly happy.

                    LARRY
          Alright! There we go. I've turned
          the world into a tabloid!

He hits a black BUTTON.

                    ALTHEA
          While you're out, pick up some
          bananas.

149   INT. HALLWAY OUTSIDE BEDROOM   149

The steel door clicks and starts GRINDING open.

                                        CUT TO:

150   EXT. MANSION - DAY   150

In the raining drench, marshals force Larry in his wheelchair
into a police van. The soaked newspeople are going berserk.

                    LARRY
          Don't let them silence me! I KNOW
          TOO MUCH!

                    REPORTER
          Are you really that scared?

                    LARRY
          No. It's just a publicity gimmick.
          And thank God you all fell for it!

He opens his coat, revealing "Larry Flynt for President" on his
shirt.

The wet reporters frown, burned.

                                        WIPE TO:

151   INT. MANTKE'S COURTROOM - DAY   151

Judge Mantke sits calmly, waiting. Suddenly the doors BURST
open, and the Larry Flynt circus barges in. Bailiffs,
marshals, lawyers, buddies, and shackled Larry HOLLERING over
the din.

                         LARRY
               Take your hands off me! These cuffs
               are too tight. OW! I'm a CRIPPLE!

Larry is rolled to the front, then brakes.

CLOSEUP - MANTKE

He stares down this menace with a horrid dread.

                                              CUT TO:

152   LATER   152

Larry is on the stand. The bailiff holds up a Bible.

                         BAILIFF
               Do you swear to tell the truth, the
               whole truth, and nothing but the
               truth, so help you God?

                         LARRY
               No.

                         MANTKE
                    (startled)
               No?

Larry abruptly removes his hand from the Bible.

                         LARRY
               I'm an Atheist. I won't swear on
               anything to God.

Mantke sighs.

                         MANTKE
               Mr. Flynt, you are a handful.
                    (overwhelmed)
               You've wreaked havoc on this DeLorean
               case, you've produced an audiotape
               which mysteriously disppears, if your
               evidence is proven factual it will
               probably produce a mistrial... Where
               will it all end?

                         LARRY
               I don't know, your Honor.

                              MANTKE
          Well I'll tell you what, Mr. Flynt.
          I'm willing to believe that this tape
          was stolen. But please, I need you
          to tell me one thing: WHO WAS THE
          SOURCE OF YOUR AUDIOTAPE?

Hmm.   Larry thinks long and hard about this, then speaks:

                              LARRY
          Well, you see, Your Honor... there
          was a girl named Vicki Morgan, who
          was Alfred Bloomingdale's mistress...

ON ISAACMAN

His face pales.

                              ISAACMAN
          Oh my God...

ON LARRY

He cheerily continues.

                              LARRY
          Now Vicki was a party girl. And when
          Alfred introduced her to Reagan's
          cabinet buddies, they liked her -- if
          you know what I mean.
                    (he winks at Mantke)
          Unfortunately, Vicki was naive enough
          to start writin' a book about these'
          sex orgies. Suddenly, BINGO -- she
          gets murdered!

                              MANTKE
                    (holding his temper)
          Mr. Flynt, how are you connected to
          this?

                              LARRY
                    (emotional)
          Your Honor, you can see I'm sittin'
          in a wheelchair! These are some of
          the same thugs who had me gunned
          down!

Mantke is mystified.

The court STENOGRAPHER keeps typing.

                          LARRY
          But, what these White House killers
          didn't realize is that Vicki
          videotaped their sexcapades. And
          these tapes are dirty, Your Honor --
          pure carnality. If our country knew
          our leaders were involved in these
          filthy activities... believe me, heads
          would roll.

                          MANTKE
          Mr. Flynt, what does this have to do
          with the DeLorean trial?

                          ISAACMAN
                        (mumbling)
          Good question...

                          LARRY
          Oh, nothin', Your Honor. It just
          made me think of it, because I have
          that tape, and this tape.

Mantke is astounded.

                          MANTKE
          Mr. Flynt, stick to the subject! Now
          who is your source?

                          LARRY
          NEVER! You wouldn't ask that to Time
          magazine. I ain't squawkin'!

                          MANTKE
          This is a court order!

                          LARRY
          With all due respect, Your Honor, you
          do not have the right to ask!!

Mantke glares. He SLAMS his gavel.

                          MANTKE
          That's it! You're in contempt.
          Beginning tomorrow, I'm fining you
          $10,000 a day until you reveal who
          gave you the tape.

                                            CUT TO:

153   EXT. SUNSET BOULEVARD - NEXT DAY   153

The Sunset Strip. Half a dozen HOOKERS in cut-offs shake their
wares on a corner.

Suddenly a long WHITE LIMO cruises up, honking an "OOGAH,
OOGAH!" horn.

The girls turn.

A tinted window rolls down, and grinning Larry sticks his head out. He's wearing a COMBAT HELMET.

> LARRY
> Hey girls, wanna make some easy
> money?

154   EXT. COURTHOUSE - DAY   154

The limo screeches up, and Larry is helped out. He wears the combat helmet, plus a Purple Heart on his bulletproof vest. REPORTERS see him and scramble over like insects.

> REPORTER
> Larry! When can we see the Vicki
> Morgan Sex Tapes?

> LARRY
> When I'm good and ready! During the
> New Hampshire Primary, I'm mailing
> 'em to every registered voter. These
> tapes will destroy the Reagan
> hypocrites!

The reporters are wowed. Arlo wheels Larry away, whispering.

> ARLO
> Hey, just between you and me -- do
> you really have the Vicki Morgan Sex
> Tapes?

> LARRY
> Of course not. They're imaginary.

Arlo LAUGHS.

> ARLO
> My God, you've got nothing!

> LARRY
> All I ever had was the FBI video.
> I paid some clerk at DeLorean's
> lawfirm five grand -- best investment
> I ever made. It gave me credibility.
> Now those idiots believe anything I
> say.

                                                CUT TO:

155   INT. MANTKE'S COURTROOM - DAY   155

Judge Mantke sternly peers at deadpan Larry.

> MANTKE
> Mr. Flynt, are you prepared to pay
> today's $10,000 fine?

> LARRY
> Yes, Your Honor.

Larry SNAPS his fingers.

The back doors swing open. And the hookers strut in, carrying
trash bags tied with pink ribbons.

The bailiff's eyes pop.

The hookers rip the bags open and dump $10,000 IN CRUMPLED
BILLS onto the floor. Larry booms.

>   LARRY
>   I am a publisher! I have a right to
>   keep the source of the tape
>   confidential under the First
>   Amendment right of freedom of the
>   press.

Mantke blinks, unimpressed.

>   MANTKE
>   What denomination are we looking at?

>   LARRY
>   One-dollar bills, Your Honor.

>   MANTKE
>   (irked)
>   Fine. Start counting.

Larry wiggles his eyebrows, then rolls forward to the money. A
dramatic pause... then he removes a shawl from his legs.

Larry is WEARING A DIAPER MADE OF THE AMERICAN FLAG.

ANGLE - MANTKE

What the fuck?! He shudders.

>   MANTKE
>   Mr. Flynt! Is that an American
>   FLAG?!

WIDE

>   LARRY
>   Yeah, I made it into a diaper.

>   MANTKE
>   WHY?!

>   LARRY
>   Since you treat me like a baby, I'm
>   gonna act like one.

Mantke throws up his hands, furious.

                    MANTKE
          Mr. Flynt, I'm arresting you for
          desecrating the American flag!
                    (he turns)
          Bailiff, take him into custody!

Isaacman leaps to attention.

                    ISAACMAN
          Your Honor, can we post bail?

                    MANTKE
          Fine. $50,000, and I'd prefer a
          cashier's check.
                    (beat)
          But I'm keeping our Mr. Flynt on a
          short leash. As a condition of his
          release, he absolutely <u>cannot leave</u>
          <u>California</u>.

                                        CUT TO:

156   INT. MANSION - NIGHT   156

     Campaign headquarters. Larry and his gang work at a GIANT U.S.
     MAP dotted with colored pins.

                    LARRY
          Okay, first we'll fly to Dallas.
          Then to Cincinnati. Then to Vegas.
          Then to Alaska.

     Althea GROANS, bleary-eyed. In a tight punk get-up, she looks
     scarily skinny.

                    ALTHEA
          Uggghhhh! I'm so fuckin' sick of
          this! It's such a waste of time...

                    LARRY
          But honey, don't you get it? I'm
          mocking the hypocrisy of the system.
          The ruling class represses free
          thought --

                    ALTHEA
          Wank off! Wank off!

                    LARRY
                    (insulted)
          You're not acting like a First Lady.

                    ALTHEA
          I don't wanna be a mother-fuckin'
          First Lady.
                    (beat)
          I'm goin' to Madame Wong's.

     Althea stumbles out the door.

Larry shakes his head, then returns to his flight plans.

> LARRY
> Well anyway, like I was sayin'...
> once we get to Alaska, we're gonna
> recreate the flight of Korean
> Airliner 007 -- find out why it was
> shot down.
> > (he draws a dotted line on the
> > map)
> See, we'll move in a north-western
> trajectory, go this way, and fly over
> Soviet airspace...

> ARLO
> Jesus Christ! Larry, you can't do
> that -- there's international laws.

> LARRY
> So what? If the Russkies blow me up,
> I'll be an American hero!

> JIMMY
> > (unimpressed)
> Yeah, but we'll be in the plane with
> you.

Suddenly -- CRASH!!!

A huge COLLISION outside.

Everybody drops their things and runs to the window. Larry
zooms over in his wheelchair.

157 OUTSIDE   157

They crowd in the window, peering down.

Below, a Rolls Royce has been plowed into a tree. The car is
upended and totalled. Althea hangs out the driver's door, her
head resting on the grass.

Larry shouts down.

> LARRY
> Babe, what happened?!

> ALTHEA
> > (blase)
> Ehh, it's hard to drive with a needle
> in your arm.

> > > > > CUT TO:

158 EST. WASHINGTON BUILDING - NIGHT   158

A looming building says "FEDERAL COMMUNICATIONS COMMISSION"

159   INT. FCC OFFICES   159

In a shadowy room, two WASHINGTON GUYS gape at a TV in horror.
They watch Larry give a speech.

> LARRY (on TV)
> Since I am a candidate, I will begin
> buying 30-minute blocks of primetime
> television, where I will explain my
> political platform... peppered with
> hot, hard-core triple X footage.
> (he smirks)
> Because as we all know, federal law
> prohibits censoring political ads.

The guys are freaked.

> WASHINGTON GUY #1
> My God! This s.o.b. has found a
> loophole.

> LARRY (on TV)
> I'm the People's Candidate! Anyone
> who's been screwed over will vote for
> me! Every poor white cracker! Every
> black! Every Jew! Every cripple!
> Every Indian! Every Hustler reader!
> I got them all! I AM the next
> President of the United States!!!

The guys stare gravely at each other.

> WASHINGTON GUY #2
> We have to stop him.

                                          CUT TO:

160   EXT. LAX AIRPORT - DAY   160

The Hustler plane WHIRS. Larry eagerly wheels toward it.

Suddenly a car RACES down the tarmac and screeches at us.
Isaacman leaps out, running to Larry and hopping alongside the
wheelchair. Larry speeds up.

> ISAACMAN
> Do NOT get on that plane! Do NOT
> leave California! The Feds are
> really pissed-off.

> LARRY
> (bizarrely irrational)
> Good!

> ISAACMAN
> Why is that good? You and I hooked
> up because we wanted to fight for the
> First Amendment -- but now... I don't
> even know WHAT you're accomplishing.

                    LARRY
          Alan, I'm just tryin' to show that
          in America, any boy can grow up to
          be President.

                    ISAACMAN
                    (irritated)
          That's bull! You're not even trying
          to win!

                    LARRY
          Lighten up. I'm a lawyer's dream
          client -- rich and always in trouble.

                    ISAACMAN
          It's not funny! Law is not a game.

Larry gets enraged. He suddenly stops.

                    LARRY
          You're RIGHT. It's A FUCKIN' JOKE!!
          Five-and-a-half years since I was
          shot, and the government still hasn't
          produced ONE SUSPECT!

                    ISAACMAN
          I know. I was there too. But you
          don't see me trying to get revenge
          on an entire country.

                    LARRY
          Alan, I can't WALK! I can't FUCK!
                    (terribly upset)
          But I got MONEY! And that gives me
          the right to make the whole corrupt
          system eat my shit.

                                             CUT TO:

161 EXT. ALASKA - NIGHT   161

     Glacier ice caps glisten below an ink black sky. The pink
     plane glides silently into view.

162 INT. HUSTLER PLANE   162

     The cockpit door opens, and a WORRIED PILOT enters.

                    WORRIED PILOT
          Excuse me, I just received a
          transmission from Anchorage Airport.
          We're being grounded.

                    LARRY
          WHY?

                         WORRIED PILOT
          The FAA saw our flight plans, and
          they tipped off the State Department
          and the Soviet Embassy. There's a
          lot of angry people saying we weren't
          authorized to fly over Russia.

                         LARRY
                    (beat)
          Curses, foiled again!

                                        CUT TO:

163   EXT. ANCHORAGE AIRPORT - NIGHT   163

Freezing snow blows in the dark. ESKIMO FEDERAL MARSHALS stand
in the cold, as the pink Hustler plane taxis to a stop. The
plane door slowly opens. The marshals lift their guns, aimed
and ready.

And then -- Larry appears in the doorway, dressed like Santa
Claus.

                                        CUT TO:

164   INT. MANTKE'S COURTROOM - DAY   164

Mantke glares incredulously. Larry is sitting there, wild-eyed
in his Santa suit. Althea watches in back, forlorn.

                         MANTKE
          Mr. Flynt, wasn't I clear? Didn't
          I explicitly state that you couldn't
          leave California?

                         ISAACMAN
          I'm sorry about the misunderstanding,
          Your Honor. Mr. Flynt always
          intended to be back in court on
          Monday --

                         LARRY
          Unless the Commies shot me down.

                         MANTKE
                    (unamused)
          That is not humorous. These added
          contempt charges are quite serious.

Larry bows his head, acting like a bad kid coming clean.

                         LARRY
          Your Honor, you're right. I realize
          that rules help us, not hurt us.
                    (coyly remorseful)
          I've learned my lesson, and now I
          want to fess up and reveal my source.

                    MANTKE
          Well -- I'm glad to hear this. I'm
          pleased you've come around.
                    (taking notes)
          Who was it?

Larry speaks, deadpan.

                    LARRY
          The Samurai.

                    MANTKE
                    (startled)
          Excuse me??

                    LARRY
          The Samurai gave me the tape.

                    MANTKE
                    (confused)
          Who is he? Where is this man?

                    LARRY
          Well, unfortunately he was critically
          injured while delivering me the tape.
          So he's receiving medical treatment
          in China.

Judge Mantke wipes his brow.

                    MANTKE
          Mr. Flynt, I fear you are mentally
          ill.

                    LARRY
          Well, opinions are like assholes.
          Everybody's got one.

Mantke CHOKES in shock.

                    ISAACMAN
          Cut it out, Larry --

                    LARRY
          Shut up, Alan.

                    MANTKE
          Mr. Flynt, listen to your lawyer.
          Let him speak for you.

                    LARRY
          I know the rules!
                    (he snaps at Isaacman)
          You're _fired_! There, now I'm my own
          lawyer. I can say whatever I want!

                    ISAACMAN
          You can't fire me. I fire you.

                         LARRY
              You can't fuckin' fire me!

                         MANTKE
              Mr. Flynt! I will NOT have cursing
              in my courtroom.

                         LARRY
              Oh. Well what about spitting??

Larry HOCKS a giant loogie and SPITS it across the room.

The Judge ducks and SLAMS his gavel.

                         MANTKE
              Bailiff! Gag that man!!

The bailiff nervously walks over, holding out ELECTRICAL TAPE.
Larry snaps his teeth threateningly and GROWLS like a mad dog.

                         LARRY
              Grrr!!!

The bailiff quickly tapes up Larry's mouth. Larry actually
freezes, caught off-guard.

Mantke stares him down.

                         MANTKE
              Mr. Flynt, are you going to calm
              down?

Surprised by this turn of events, Larry nods, Harpo-like.

                         MANTKE
              Are you going to create any more
              nonsense in my courtroom?

Larry shakes his head.

                         MANTKE
              If I ungag you, do you promise to
              show me and my staff the courtesy
              they deserve?

Larry imploringly nods.

Mantke sighs, then signals the bailiff. The bailiff hesitantly
RIPS the tape off Larry's face.

Larry howls in pain, then in retaliation throws an ORANGE at
the bailiff, CLONKING him.

The Judge blows a fuse.

                              MANTKE
                         (outraged)
                    I've had ENOUGH OF THIS! Mr. Flynt,
                    you leave me no choice but to
                    sentence you to nine months --

                              LARRY
                    That's all ya got?! GIVE ME MORE!

                              MANTKE
                    Fine. I'll add another six months!

                              LARRY
                    GOOD!

Althea winces. Larry suddenly catches himself.

                              LARRY
                    Uh-oh --

He looks frantically at Isaacman. Isaacman mutters.

                              ISAACMAN
                    Ask to post bail.

                              LARRY
                    Okay. Your Honor, can I post bail?

CLOSEUP - MANTKE

A pause. And then --

                              MANTKE
                    NO.
                         (he glowers powerfully)
                    Larry Flynt, you are hereby sentenced
                    to fifteen months... in federal
                    psychiatric prison.
                         (beat)
                    Now get him out of my courtroom.

CLOSEUP - LARRY

Absolute shock. The color drains from his face.

WIDE

Then THREE BAILIFFS sneak up behind and grab the wheelchair.
Larry tries pushing them away. They push back. A scuffle
breaks out. Finally they restrain him, and the wheelchair gets
rolled backwards and disappears out of the courtroom.

Althea stares, pained.

                                                  CUT TO:

165   EST. SPRINGFIELD FEDERAL PRISON - DAY   165

A dark, spooky fortress with high fence containing it.

166   INT. SPRINGFIELD - DAY   166

The prison psychiatric unit. Dim corridors buzz with
flickering fluorescents.

Terrifying muffled SCREAMS echo off the walls.

PRISONERS in straitjackets bang their heads in padded cells.

Larry gets rolled in, chained to a gurney. He is shivering,
clammy, and seems completely disoriented.

Larry is in hell.

                                              CUT TO:

167   EST. LIBERTY BAPTIST COLLEGE - DAY   167

A quaint, lovely school on thousands of green Virginia acres.
A cross stands high above.

168   INT. COLLEGE CORRIDOR - DAY   168

A clean-cut DIVINITY STUDENT marches formally down a long
subdued hallway. Paintings of Jesus pass by.

The young man gulps nervously.

Clutched tightly in his hand is a copy of HUSTLER.

169   INT. DEAN'S OFFICE - DAY   169

A proper, RESERVED DEAN is working. Jesus hangs on the cross
behind him. The young man KNOCKS and tentatively enters.

                    DIVINITY STUDENT
          Sir, I'm so sorry to disturb you --
          but I have something quite...
                (searching for the word)
          odious you need to be aware of.

He gingerly places the Hustler down. On the cover, two women
French kiss.

The Dean raises an eyebrow. The student opens the magazine,
revealing the FULL-PAGE CAMPARI AD PARODY. Jerry Falwell's
picture stares out. The Dean is befuddled.

                    DEAN
          I don't understand. The Reverend
          would never endorse a liquor
          company...

                    DIVINITY STUDENT
          Well... there's a larger problem.
          Ahem. Substantially larger.
                (nervous)
          It says the Reverend fornicated with
          his mother in an outhouse.

The Dean's eyes pop.

                                        CUT TO:

A DOOR

Stenciled lettering says "Reverend Jerry Falwell, Chancellor"

170   INT. FALWELL'S OFFICE   170

A dignified office for an important man. Photos of Falwell
with Reagan, Bush, and Bob Dole litter the walls. Sitting at
a desk, intently reading his Bible, is the REVEREND JERRY
FALWELL. Formidable, dedicated, strong-willed, he truly sees
himself as an anointed leader of a Godly Moral Majority.

Falwell glances up.

                    REV. FALWELL
          Give me a second.

Falwell finishes reading the Bible passage. Finally finished,
he places a ribbon on the page and shuts the Book.

Falwell smiles warmly.

                    REV. FALWELL
          So what do you boys got for me?

The Dean and the Student stand across from him. They look ill.

                    DEAN
          Uh, Reverend... I think you should
          read this.

He hands Falwell the Hustler AD.

Falwell innocently examines it.

FALWELL'S POV

A blizzard of TERRIBLE WORDS leap out at us:

 "Mom"

                              "Shit"

      "Flies"

                         "Campari in the crapper"

   "Kicked the goat out"

                         "Baptist whore"

    "Passed out before I could come"

CLOSEUP - FALWELL

He turns frighteningly pale. All color, all emotion, all life
just drains from his face.

He whispers faintly.

                         REV. FALWELL
              Dear Lord...

                                              CUT TO:

171   INT. SPRINGFIELD PRISON - DAY   171

      Larry sits in a padded cell. He hasn't been shaved in days,
      and his eyes are glazed and lifeless. A glob of drool hangs
      from his open mouth.

      Outside, keys clank, and the cell door gets unlocked and flung
      open. A muscular ORDERLY stares passively.

                         ORDERLY
              Flynt. You've got a visitor.

      Larry GRUNTS.

172   INT. PRISON VISITOR CHECK-IN - DAY   172

      Gaunt, withered Althea struggles to stand as a GUARD frisks
      her. Absurdly, he pats down her skeletal frame.

173   VISITORS AREA   173

      Larry sits glumly, overweight like a blob of dough. Behind a
      GLASS WALL, Althea staggers over and plunks down. She catches
      her breath.

                         ALTHEA
              You look good...

      He stares unresponsively, quite over-medicated.

                         LARRY
              Mrmmm...

                         ALTHEA
                    (awkward)
              Lar', I got some bad news...

                         LARRY
              Mrhm...

      She realizes this is all she's gonna get from him. Althea
      starts crying.

                              ALTHEA
                    Larry... I don't want to work at the
                    magazine anymore...
                              (crying harder)
                    Some people there... won't even shake
                    my hand...

                              LARRY
                    Mrmuhhh?

                              ALTHEA
                    ...I got AIDS...

Larry gazes. He's probably comprehending, but doesn't speak.

Althea leans up to the glass.

                              ALTHEA
                    Do you understand...?

TIGHT - LARRY

A pause. His eyes drop, overwhelmed.

Then, shuddering, he struggles and lifts his hand to the glass.
Althea places her hand against it.

                              LARRY
                    Won't even shake your haaaand...?

                                                  CUT TO:

174   INT. HUSTLER OFFICES - DAY   174

Somber staffers work. A cute RECEPTIONIST answers the phone.

                              RECEPTIONIST
                    Larry Flynt Publications.
                              (suddenly surprised)
                    Oh! Yes Sir!
                              (she snatches a MICROPHONE)
                    CODE PINK! CODE PINK!

Her voice gets AMPLIFIED all over. Everyone leaps from their
desks and scurries crazily.

175   INT. CONFERENCE ROOM   175

Everybody hastily gathers around the table. A SPEAKER PHONE is
placed in the center. They all stare at it, waiting...

Finally -- Larry's drugged, confused-sounding VOICE barks out.

                              LARRY'S VOICE
                    Is everybody therrre...?

                              JIMMY
                    Yeah, Larry. We're all here. So,
                    uh -- how are you?

                         LARRY'S VOICE
          Never you mind about that... I have
          some import'nt announcements to
          maaaake....
                    (a long pause)
          First... I wanna withdrawww my
          candidacy for Prezident...

The group is startled.

                         STAFFER
          Why?!

                         LARRY'S VOICE
                    (suddenly enraged)
          Never you mind why! It's none of yer
          fuckin' business!!
                    (beat)
          But take all them t-shirts and bumper
          stickers, and BURN 'EM! Just toss
          'em in the incinerator! The carnival
          is closed.

Everybody is astonished.

                         LARRY'S VOICE
          Okay. Next point of biziness.
          Chester, Morgan, Stephanie, Timmy,
          Bruce, Arlo... y'all there?

                         STAFFERS
                    (in unison)
          Yes, Larry.

                         LARRY'S VOICE
          Good. You're all fired.

HUH? People are flabbergasted. Jimmy jumps up.

                         JIMMY
          Larry, you can't do this! We need
          these people.

                         LARRY'S VOICE
          Shut up, Jimbo. It's my business,
          and I'll run it into the ground if
          I want to!!
                    (pause)
          Okay, that's all. I gotta go.

CLICK. He suddenly hangs up. A DIAL TONE comes on.

Everybody keeps staring at the speaker phone, totally weirded
out. It's like they're expecting Larry to jump out of it.

                         ARLO
          What the fuck was that?!

                         CHESTER
          Maybe I can get a job at Mad Magazine --

                         JIMMY
          CALM DOWN! Don't everybody panic.
          You're not fired.

                         STAFFER
          But Larry just said --

                         JIMMY
          Yeah, well Larry's in a <u>nuthouse</u>,
          ain't he?

Hmm. Not a bad point.

                                        CUT TO:

176   INT. ISAACMAN'S LAWFIRM - DAY   176

      Isaacman is calmly working. Suddenly -- the INTERCOM.

                         SECRETARY'S VOICE
          Mr. Isaacman, you have a visitor...
                    (unsettled)
          She has no appointment... it's Mrs.
          Flynt.

He looks up, surprised. Suddenly the door flies open -- and
standing there is sick Althea, being held up by two bodyguards.
She looks sad and shrunken.

Isaacman's face drops.

                         ISAACMAN
          Althea...

The bodyguards gingerly carry Althea in, her feet pantomiming
walking on air. They put her on the couch. She uncomfortably
adjusts herself, then signals them to leave.

Silence. Alan and Althea peer uncertainly at each other.

                         ISAACMAN
          Long time no see...

Althea nods, then struggles and pulls a PACKET of stapled
papers from her purse.

                         ALTHEA
          Alan... this came for Larry...

Isaacman examines the papers. His eyes widen in disbelief.

                         ISAACMAN
          Whoa.

                         ALTHEA
          Pretty intense, huh?

ISAACMAN
(frowning)
Yep...

ALTHEA
So what are you gonna do?

ISAACMAN
(awkward)
Althea... I'm not your lawyer
anymore. Larry fired me.

Voice wavering, Althea shrugs.

ALTHEA
You know Larry...
(very soft)
Alan... please help me.

Isaacman rubs his face tiredly. Is he up for Round Ten?

CUT TO:

177   INT. LARRY'S PRISON CELL - DAY   177

Larry peers up sideways from his gurney. Frazzled Isaacman
enters the cell.

ISAACMAN
(sarcastically sing-song)
Hello, Larry. Remember me?

Larry nods and gestures, a parody of etiquette: Please sit.

ISAACMAN
Oh -- thank you.
(he sits)
I didn't expect to find myself
here... but you got a letter from the
Reverend Jerry Falwell. He saw your
Campari ad -- and even though it said
"Parody, Not To Be Taken Seriously"
-- he wasn't amused. Fact is, he was
infuriated.

Larry's face lights up -- how delightful.

ISAACMAN
So he's filed suit, charging you with
Libel and Intentional Infliction of
Emotional Distress. You're being
sued for 45 million dollars!

Larry's smirk drops.

                    ISAACMAN
          Falwell's so pissed, he sent a
          million letters to his Moral Majority
          flock, hitting them up for money to
          fight you in court and send you back
          to hell.
                    (beat)
          He's even enclosed a copy of the ad,
          to really upset them!
                    (he leans in)
          So, look, I know your medication
          makes it tough for you to talk...
          but... do you want me to do anything?

CLOSEUP - LARRY

A long pause. His chest fills with air, and then a single word
crawls slowly up his throat and pops out of his mouth:

                    LARRY
          Countersue.

                                                  CUT TO:

178   INT. TV STUDIOS - DAY   178

The studios for the "Old Time Gospel Hour." TECHNICIANS scurry
around a glitzy set with a lectern. A makeup girl is touching
up Reverend Falwell. Suddenly he yelps out in shock.

                    REV. FALWELL
          WHAT??!!!!!!!!!!

His ponderous, puffed-up lawyer ROY GRUTMAN tries to appease
him.

                    GRUTMAN
          Uh, yeah... Jerry... he's suing you.

                    REV. FALWELL
          He's suing ME???!!
                    (baffled)
          For heaven's sake, why?!!!

                    GRUTMAN
                    (he winces)
          Copyright infringement. You xeroxed
          his ad, and raised money with it.

Falwell turns red with rage.

                    REV. FALWELL
          His depth of depravity sickens me!
          He is LUCIFER!

179   INT. KEATING'S OFFICE - DAY   179

A giant cabinet is opened -- and it's stuffed with SHELVES OF
PORN. Racks and racks of Hustlers, Penthouses, videos, etc.
Charles Keating's hands pull out the Hustlers.

                    CHARLES KEATING (o.s.)
               I've kept meticulous records. Any
               research problems, you're encouraged
               to use my archives.

We WIDEN. Keating is showing the magazines to Grutman.

                    CHARLES KEATING
               And tell the Reverend that I've dealt
               with this filthmonger myself. I wish
               to offer my support.

Grutman nods and begins perusing a Hustler. Suddenly, his eyes
bug out.

                    GRUTMAN
               Is that the Tin Man?

                                             CUT TO:

180   EXT. SPRINGFIELD FEDERAL PRISON - DAY   180

Isaacman waits next to a prison van. Suddenly Larry gets
rolled over by armed GUARDS. His hands are cuffed and strapped
down, his scraggly beard is real scummy, and his suspicious
eyes dart about like a caged animal.

Isaacman frowns. He watches Larry get loaded on the van lift.

181   INT. PRISON VAN - MOVING   181

                    ISAACMAN
               I do wish you had shaved. We're
               going to court.

                    LARRY
                 (speech slurred)
               Listen... I didn't get my breakfast,
               they forgot my enema, nobody cleaned
               my bedsore, and Jimmy thinks I'm
               crazy -- he's tryin' to become my
               conservator.

Isaacman winces. Larry is a seriously ornery son-of-a-bitch.

                    ISAACMAN
               Well, let's not worry about these
               things. Let's talk about your
               testimony. All that matters is that
               the jury understands it's satire --
               the ad's too ridiculous to believe.
                 (more)

                    ISAACMAN (Cont'd)
                (beat)
        Just go up on the stand, give 'em a
        friendly smile, and say it was a
        joke. You were simply pokin' fun at
        the Reverend.

Larry thinks.

                    LARRY
        I'm just a clown.

                    ISAACMAN
        Exactly!

Larry scowls.

                                        CUT TO:

182 INT. U.S. DISTRICT COURTHOUSE - ROANOKE, VIRGINIA - DAY   182

The big trial.

In a packed courtroom, Jerry Falwell is on the stand
testifying. Grutman paces pompously. JUDGE JAMES TURK
watches.

                    REV. FALWELL
        ...I have a number of honorary
        degrees. I have been named
        "Clergyman of the Year." I have been
        awarded "Humanitarian of the Year"...

                    GRUTMAN
        Has the Good Housekeeping Poll of
        influential Americans ever included
        you?

                    REV. FALWELL
        Yes. Last year, I was second most-
        admired, behind the President.

Falwell speaks confidently. The TWELVE JURORS are impressed.

But Larry glares menacingly. Isaacman whispers.

                    ISAACMAN
        That's good for us. It just makes
        him a bigger target.

Grutman strides to a large blow-up of the CAMPARI AD, sitting
on an easel. He gestures with a pointer.

                    GRUTMAN
        Mr. Falwell, I'd like to draw your
        attention to Exhibit One.
                (more)

                    GRUTMAN (Cont'd)
The caption reads: "Jerry Falwell
talks about his first time" -- and
there appears to be a photograph of
you. Did you give consent for the
use of your name or photograph in
this ad?

                    REV. FALWELL
I did not.

                    GRUTMAN
               (he nods)
All right. Underneath your
photograph, it reads, quote --
"FALWELL: My first time was in an
outhouse outside Lynchburg, Virginia.
I never _really_ expected to make it
with Mom, but then after she showed
all of the other guys in town such
a good time, I figured, 'What the
hell.'" Unquote.
               (he looks up)
Now, referring to the use of the verb
"make it," according to your
interpretation, Mr. Falwell, did that
have a sexual connotation?

                    REV. FALWELL
               (awkward)
That... is street vernacular for
sexual intercourse.

Falwell holds his dignified pose.

Larry cracks a dirty smile.

                    GRUTMAN
Next, quote -- "INTERVIEWER: But your
mom? Isn't that a bit odd?"
"FALWELL: I don't think so. Looks
don't mean that much to me in a
woman." Unquote.

Yikes. The jurors grimace uncomfortably.

Isaacman squirms in his seat, wanting Grutman to move on.

Grutman milks the stink in the air, then gently continues.

                    GRUTMAN
Did you ever say that?

                    REV. FALWELL
Never.

> GRUTMAN
> Please tell us, Mr. Falwell, what was
> the nature of the relationship
> between you and your mother?

> REV. FALWELL
> We were as close as a mother and son
> could be on this earth. She was a
> very godly woman... probably the
> closest to a saint that I have ever
> known.

Larry scowls. Grutman gingerly continues.

> GRUTMAN
> Forgive this question -- but I must
> ask it... was your mother anyone who
> ever committed incest?

Isaacman LEAPS from his chair, objecting.

> ISAACMAN
> Your Honor! Excuse me, it seems to
> me that we could certainly stipulate
> that his mother was a person of the
> finest moral character, and that she
> is now deceased, and that this really
> is not necessary --

> JUDGE
> (cutting him off)
> I'll let him answer the question.

ANGLE - GRUTMAN

He hides his pleasure. Here comes the Big Out-Of-The-Ballpark,
Bases-Loaded Moment.

> GRUTMAN
> Mr. Falwell, specifically... did you
> and your mother ever commit incest?

CLOSEUP - FALWELL

Such agony. He bites his lip, pained.

> REV. FALWELL
> Absolutely not.

WIDE

The jury shake their heads. How ugly.

Falwell glances at Larry -- and their eyes lock. Time stops.
Larry and Jerry. Jerry and Larry. Nobody else exists.
Falwell gravely holds his emotions.

But Larry burns -- a timebomb about to explode.

                                                    CUT TO:

183 LATER   183

Larry is on the stand. Grutman smugly approaches.

                    GRUTMAN
          Mr. Flynt, will you please state your
          full name?

                    LARRY
          My name is Christopher Columbus
          Cornwallis I.P.Q. Harvey H. And Pagey
          Pui.

Isaacman grimaces. Grutman is unamused.

                    GRUTMAN
          Are you known as Larry Flynt?

                    LARRY
          No.   Jesus H. Flynt, Esquire.

                    GRUTMAN
          Are you the publisher and editor-
          in-chief for Hustler magazine?

                    LARRY
          Yep, I put out the most tasteless,
          sleaziest, greatest porn magazine in
          the world!

Grutman lifts a piece of TYPED PAPER off the exhibit table.

                    GRUTMAN
          Alright. I have here Exhibit B, a
          typewritten script of the Campari ad
          copy. There are approval initials
          from the legal department, and then
          "Okay, L.F." What does that mean?

                    LARRY
          It means they could take it to the
          bank.

                    GRUTMAN
          And when you approved this ad, did
          you have any knowledge specifically
          that Reverend Falwell had ever had
          intercourse with his mother?

A pause. Larry gazes at Falwell.

                    LARRY
          Yes.

                    GRUTMAN
                 (startled)
     What??

                    LARRY
     YES.

Isaacman's jaw drops.

Falwell's jaw drops further.

The crowd goes CRAZY.

                    LARRY
          I have an affidavit signed by three
          people stating that they witnessed
          the incestuous act.

                    GRUTMAN
          You DO??
                 (bewildered)
          And... where is this affidavit?

                    LARRY
          It's locked in an airtight vault
          where nobody can meddle with it.

                    GRUTMAN
          Mr. Flynt, you're making this all up.

                    LARRY
                 (insulted)
          No, I'm not. The affidavit states
          that the incident was observed by
          three boys peeking through the window
          of the outhouse.

Isaacman tries to intercept.

                    ISAACMAN
          Your Honor!
                 (to the Judge)
          Just to make something clear, we are
          not aware of any such documentation --

                    LARRY
          BRAVO NOVEMBER. BRAVO WHISKEY.

                    GRUTMAN
          Mr. Flynt?

Larry is receiving radio signals.

                    LARRY
          ELEVEN BRAVO.

                    GRUTMAN
          Mr. Flynt --

                    LARRY
          (talking into a pretend mike)
YOU'RE CLEARED FOR RUNWAY TWO. CAN
YOU GIVE ME AN E.T.A. ON IT?

                    GRUTMAN
Mr. Flynt, can we get back on the
subject?!

Larry snaps back.

                    LARRY
And <u>ya know what</u>?? There's somethin'
else in that vault: A photo of Jerry
having coitus with a sheep.
          (he gets indignant)
And <u>no one</u> has the right of taking
the individual liberty of sticking
their sexual organ in some poor
animal's mouth! Now, there's a big
difference between civil rights and
individual liberties. And you should
learn the difference. I mean, an
individual liberty is something I'd
like to do right now -- take a shit
right on top of your head. But civil
rights is what's been violated by
locking me in a hellhole psychiatric
prison.

Grutman tries to regain control.

                    GRUTMAN
Mr. Flynt, do you realize by
publishing this ad parody, you were
conveying to the reader that Reverend
Falwell was just as you characterized
him -- a liar?

                    LARRY
He's a liar and a glutton.

                    GRUTMAN
You wanted to hold him up to
ridicule?

                    LARRY
No, contempt.

                    GRUTMAN
Contempt. Scorn?

                    LARRY
Truculent.

                    GRUTMAN
Obloquy?

                    LARRY
          Parlez-vous francais?

                    GRUTMAN
          Je parle le francais mieux que toi.

                    LARRY
          Oui, je veux vais coucher vous, avec
          vous -- I'm sorry, it's rusty, Jesus
          Christ, it is rusty.

                    GRUTMAN
          Mr. Flynt, do you have an aversion
          to organized religion?

                    LARRY
          You bet your sweet ass I do.

                    GRUTMAN
          Do you believe that gives you license
          to mock leaders of religious
          movements?

                    LARRY
          You're goddamn right.

                    ISAACMAN
          OBJECTION. It's irrelevant --

                    JUDGE
          Overruled.

                    LARRY
          Free expression is absolute.

Grutman bears in.

                    GRUTMAN
          You wanted to make Reverend Falwell
          out to be a hypocrite?

                    LARRY
          Yeah.

                    GRUTMAN
          That's what you wanted to convey?

                    LARRY
          Yeah.

                    GRUTMAN
          But didn't it occur to you, that for
          Reverend Falwell to function in his
          livelihood, he has to have an
          integrity that people believe in?

                    LARRY
          Yeah.

                         GRUTMAN
          And wasn't one of your objectives to
          destroy that integrity, or harm it,
          if you could?

CLOSEUP - LARRY

                         LARRY
          To assassinate it.

                                        CUT TO:

184 EXT. COURTHOUSE - DAY   184

     Larry is squeezed wriggling into a straitjacket and thrown into
     the police van. He looks insane.

     Isaacman stands at the top of the courthouse stairs, staring
     silently at this spectacle. He looks nauseous. Finally, too
     weak to stand, he sits down and sticks his head between his legs.

                                        CUT TO:

185 INT. COURTROOM - DAY   185

                         JUDGE
          Have you reached a verdict?

                         JURY FOREWOMAN
          Yes we have, your honor.

     The BAILIFF takes a folded piece of paper from the forewoman
     and hands it to the judge.

     The judge opens the paper -- then does a startled doubletake.

                                        CUT TO:

186 INT. COURTHOUSE CORRIDOR - DAY   186

     The courtroom doors BANG open. A MOB OF REPORTERS scrambles
     out and races for the phone booths. They're freaked out.

                         REPORTER #1 (on phone)
          It's a disastrous decision! He's not
          guilty of libel, but he is guilty of
          inflicting emotional distress!

                         REPORTER #2 (on phone)
          Nobody thought the ad was real, but
          it hurt Falwell's feelings. So now
          Flynt has to pay him 200 grand!

187 INT. TIME MAGAZINE - DAY   187

     "TIME" EDITORS stare at a battery of TV sets. Almost every
     channel has Jerry Falwell's press conference.

                    REV. FALWELL (on TV)
          This ruling shows that nobody can
          prostitute the First Amendment. I
          just hope it'll set some form of
          limit in the press for people like
          Larry Flynt.

                    TIME EDITOR
          But that's where censorship <u>starts</u>
          -- with people like Larry Flynt!

188   INT. NEW YORK TIMES - DAY   188

      The same situation: Angry EDITORS watch TV sets.

                    N.Y. TIMES EDITOR
          This decision is an end run around
          the Constitution! It's for people
          who have libel suits, but know they
          can't win!

189   INT. NATIONAL LAMPOON - DAY   189

      More upset EDITORS.

                    LAMPOON EDITOR
          With this ruling, Teddy Kennedy could
          sue Art Buchwald! Nixon could sue
          every cartoonist that insulted him!
                    (he imitates Nixon)
          "When I see that big nose, I'm a
          basket case for the rest of the day!"

                                        CUT TO:

190   EXT. SPRINGFIELD PRISON YARD - DAY   190

      In front of massive prison gates, Larry sits decrepit in his
      wheelchair. Two GUARDS flank his sides.

                    GUARD
          Big day for you, Larry. You're
          gettin' out, <u>and</u> you made the front
          page.

                    LARRY
                    (glum)
          Who gives a fuck?

      The gates silently swing open.

      A limo is waiting. The guards roll Larry to the prison edge...
      then a limo DRIVER takes the chair and rolls him to the car.
      He awkwardly helps Larry in.

191   INT. LIMO - SAME TIME   191

      The door shuts. Larry turns, and he's sitting alone with
      Althea. She looks pale, sunken-cheeked, gravely ill.

Larry tries to smile.

> LARRY
> Hey, cutie-pie.

He gently kisses her.

> ALTHEA
> (voice hoarse)
> We make quite a team. A cripple
> gettin' out of a nuthouse, and a
> junkie with AIDS.

> LARRY
> Yeah... but a good-lookin' junkie.

She smiles weakly.

They cuddle tightly.

CUT TO:

192   INT. HUSTLER OFFICES - DAY   192

Staffers work busily. Suddenly -- somebody notices something
odd and turns. They all slowly glance over their shoulders...
and <u>Larry</u> is sitting in the doorway.

> LARRY
> (poker face)
> I thought I fired you all.

Nervous laughter. Nobody knows what to expect.

> LARRY
> Is Jimmy here...?

Uh-oh.

People jerk, anxiously. Larry scans the room, finally spotting
Jimmy. He points. Jimmy shudders nervously.

> JIMMY
> Uh, yeah, Larry...?

> LARRY
> Come here! Come closer...

Jimmy takes little baby steps. Larry gestures insistently from
the wheelchair. Jimmy slowly leans down... unsure if an act
of horrible violence is about to break out...

> JIMMY
> Uh, yeah... look... sorry if I tried
> to run things... but I just wanted
> to protect you from yourself...

Jimmy grimaces remorsefully. Larry pulls him to his body --
then hugs him.

> LARRY
> Don't sweat it, bro'. I forgive you.

                                        CUT TO:

193   INT. FLYNT MANSION - NIGHT   193

Larry and Althea lie in bed, like a still life. The curtains
are drawn, and he cradles her head. Suddenly she coughs.

> LARRY
> You alright? You need something?

> ALTHEA
> No. This is fine...
> (softly)
> Actually, I could use a glass of
> water.

They both look over. The WATER PITCHER is across the room.

Hmm. They slowly glance at each other.

> ALTHEA
> Oh, uh... I'll ring the maid.

> LARRY
> (chivalrously)
> No, don't worry, 'hon... I'll get
> it for you.

With much effort, Larry lifts his legs and struggles into the
wheelchair. Then he rolls across the room, reaches the water,
and pours a glass.

> ALTHEA
> Larry, when I die... I want you to
> freeze my body. Bring me back to
> life when you can cure me.

> LARRY
> Sure... Hell, I'll do it too! Then
> they can thaw us both out in the year
> 3000. We'll fuck on the moon.

He carefully balances the glass on his lap and rolls back over
to Althea. Smiling lovingly, he gives her the water.

She drinks.

> LARRY
> You're shivering...

> ALTHEA
> Maybe I'll take a bath.

She painfully sits up. Larry stares into her eyes.

                              LARRY
                    You want a ride...?

A beat. Althea is momentarily confused -- but then understands
and smiles sweetly. She climbs onto Larry's lap, and he rolls
them toward the bathroom. But suddenly -- he makes an
unexpected turn and starts going in circles, round and round
the room.

Althea laughs and hugs Larry.

Finally he stops at the bathroom. She tentatively gets off,
leaning on a counter, then kisses Larry. Althea turns and
enters the bathroom. The door shuts.

ANGLE - LARRY

He smiles after her. Then... he thinks.

We hear RUNNING WATER.

Larry rolls to the corner. He huddles over the telephone and
dials a number. When he finally talks, it's hushed,
desperate...

                              LARRY (on phone)
                    Dr. Lamont? It's Larry Flynt.
                              (pause)
                    She seems really weak.
                              (pause)
                    Look, what would it take to save her?
                    I'll write as big a check as you
                    need...
                              (longer pause)
                    I'll do anything... Can't all that
                    money save one life...?

We MOVE IN. The voice on the line says something... and
Larry's face falls.

A beat -- then Larry notices wetness under his feet. Puzzled,
he glances over. WATER is streaming under the bathroom door.

                              LARRY
                    Althea...?
                              (beat)
                    ALTHEA!!

Shit. Adrenalin shoots through his body. Larry suddenly grabs
his wheelchair wheels and hurls himself across the room. Heart
pounding, he breaks through the bathroom door.

CLOSEUP - LARRY

And he gasps.

ANGLE - THE BATHTUB

Althea is submerged in the tub, lifeless. Her hair floats
around her head like a dark halo.

CLOSEUP - LARRY

He desperately tries to pull her out, but with his dead legs,
he only falls from the chair. Overcome, Larry starts sobbing.

                                            CUT TO:

194 EXT. CEMETERY - DAY   194

Her funeral. Under a grey sky, Larry and the Hustler gang
somberly watch Althea's casket get lowered into the ground.

Nobody speaks.

Larry sits in his wheelchair, dressed in black, staring in
agonized disbelief.

Finally, he takes a single white rose and tosses it onto the
casket. A beat. Then, a voice...

                    REV. FALWELL (v.o.)
               You cannot mock God! You cannot fool
               God!

                                            CUT TO:

195 INT. MANSION BEDROOM - NIGHT   195

Larry is alone in the big house. He stares at his TV. On the
screen, Jerry Falwell is lecturing.

                    REV. FALWELL (on TV)
               If you break His laws, God Almighty
               will judge you!

Larry glares, a rage building.

                    REV. FALWELL (on TV)
               AIDS is a plague. These perverted
               lifestyles have to stop! When you
               violate moral laws, you reap the
               whirlwind.

TIGHT - LARRY

Infuriated, he suddenly EXPLODES -- a volcanic, incensed
passion we haven't seen in a hell of a long time.

Suddenly motivated, Larry snatches the telephone and furiously
punches in a number.

                              LARRY
          Alan! GET OVER HERE!

                                              CUT TO:

196   INT. MANSION DEN - LATER   196

Larry is bellowing at Isaacman.

                              LARRY
          I wanna appeal the Falwell case!

                              ISAACMAN
                    (surprised)
          But Larry -- the appeal was denied...

                              LARRY
          So go HIGHER!

                              ISAACMAN
          C'mon, the only thing higher is the
          Supreme Court.

                              LARRY
          So give 'em a call!

                              ISAACMAN
                    (he sighs)
          Larry... it's not that easy.
          Thousands of people petition every
          year...

                              LARRY
          But my case is as good as any!

An awkward moment. Isaacman takes a breath.

                              ISAACMAN
          Look -- why would they pick you?
          You're a nightmare. They're scared
          that if they let you in, you'll wear
          a diaper, or throw an orange, or
          bring a bunch of hookers.
                    (beat)
          You don't understand courtroom
          behavior. To them, you're a pig.

Larry ponders this.

                              LARRY
          But that shouldn't matter. It's the
          principle. In this country, doesn't
          a pig have the same rights as the
          president?

                    ISAACMAN
                 (frustrated)
          Yeah... Look, Larry -- every
          lawyer's dream is to go to the
          Supreme Court. A win there can
          change our country.
                 (beat)
          But your sentimental speeches and
          cornball patriotism don't work on me
          anymore. I don't believe you. Do
          you realize how many times you've
          convinced me to fight for your grand
          ideals -- only to fuck me over and
          let the ideals go down the sewer?

                    LARRY
          I know. Alan, I look back at my
          life... and I just see a path of
          destruction. I've wasted my talents,
          without doin' anything really
          important. Well, maybe this Falwell
          case is my chance.
                 (he lowers his voice)
          So you go and get me to the Supreme
          Court. Please. And I promise I'll
          behave.

Isaacman stares.

                                          CUT TO:

197 EXT. UNITED STATES SUPREME COURT - MORNING   197

The majesty of the nation's highest court. People are
arriving, climbing the towering stairs.

A TV REPORTER does a standup.

                    REPORTER
          God versus the Devil. America's
          Minister versus America's Pimp.
          Today is the showdown.
                 (beat)
          Many were surprised by the high
          court's decision to hear Larry
          Flynt's case. But he had unlikely
          supporters filing briefs on his
          behalf: The New York Times, The
          Magazine Publishers Association, The
          American Newspaper Publishers
          Association...

Cars pull up, and REPORTERS scramble over. A modest sedan
arrives -- and it's Jerry Falwell. Then a limo arrives -- and
it's Larry Flynt and Isaacman, smiling nervously. Then a
stretch limo arrives -- and it's Charles Keating.

Then a super-stretch limo arrives. Pause... and it's Larry's
parents. The reporters are baffled.

                            REPORTER
And who are you?

                            MA FLYNT
                (she smiles)
I'm Larry's mama. He flew us in all
the way from Kentucky...!

Larry turns -- and catches Falwell's eye. A beat. Then
Falwell shakes his head and quickly hurries up the stairs.
Larry peers after him.

198   INT. U.S. SUPREME COURT - DAY   198

The most important courtroom in the land.

The majestic red velvet curtains part. Then, in inspiring
ceremony, the NINE JUSTICES grandly file out. A hush comes
over the crowded room. The COURT MARSHAL stands and proclaims.

                       COURT MARSHAL
All rise! Oyez, oyez, oyez. The
Honorable, the Chief Justice and the
Associate Justices of the Supreme
Court of the United States. All
persons having business before this
honorable Court are admonished to
draw nigh and give their attention,
for the Court is now sitting. God
save the United States and this
honorable Court.

The Justices step from behind their seats and sit. All the
spectators do likewise. Chief Justice Rehnquist shuffles
through his papers.

                 CHIEF JUSTICE REHNQUIST
We'll hear the argument first this
morning in number 86-1278, Hustler
Magazine and Larry C. Flynt versus
Jerry Falwell.
                (he nods at Isaacman)
Mr. Isaacman, you may proceed
whenever you're ready.

Isaacman glances over. Larry gives him a big grin -- then
mimes zipping his lips closed.

Isaacman smiles. He stands, staring down the panel of
Justices. This is his day. Presenting himself in a low-key,
ingratiating manner, he begins.

                      ISAACMAN
Mr. Chief Justice, and may it please
the Court. One of the most cherished
interests that we have as a nation
is uninhibited debate and freedom of
speech.
                (more)

                    ISAACMAN (Cont'd)
          There is a public interest in
          allowing every citizen of this
          country to express his views.

                    JUSTICE STEVENS
          Well what view was expressed by
          Exhibit A?

                    ISAACMAN
          Uh... in the first place, it's a
          parody of a Campari ad.

                    JUSTICE STEVENS
               (deadpan)
          I understand.

                    ISAACMAN
          And it is also a satire of Jerry
          Falwell, and he is in many respects
          the perfect candidate for this,
          because he's such a ridiculous figure
          to be in a liquor ad: Somebody we're
          used to seeing standing on a pulpit,
          with a beatific look on his face,
          holding a Bible.

                    JUSTICE STEVENS
               (unrelenting)
          But what is the public interest that
          you're describing? That there's some
          interest in making him look
          ludicrous?

Isaacman pauses, cockily. He knows this is his moment.

                    ISAACMAN
          There is a public interest in having
          Hustler express its view that what
          Jerry Falwell says, as the ad parody
          indicates... is "B.S."
               (pleased at his nerve)
          And Hustler has every right to say
          that somebody who's out there
          campaigning against it, saying don't
          read our magazine and we're poison
          on the minds of America and don't
          fornicate and don't drink liquor --
          Hustler has every right to say that
          man is full of "B.S." Let's deflate
          this stuffed shirt and bring him down
          to our level.

Larry chuckles. Isaacman smiles impishly. A few Justices
laugh, getting his point.

                    JUSTICE SCALIA
        But Mr. Isaacman, the First Amendment
        is not everything. It's a very
        important value, but it's not the
        only value in our society. What
        about another value -- which is that
        good people should be able to enter
        public life and public service. The
        rule you give us says that if you
        stand for public office, or become
        a public figure in any way, you
        cannot protect yourself or, indeed,
        your mother, against a parody of your
        committing incest with her in an
        outhouse. Now, do you think George
        Washington would have stood for
        public office if that was the
        consequence?

Isaacman is relaxed, warmed-up. He's prepped for this
question.

                    ISAACMAN
        Well, there's a 200-year-old cartoon
        -- I think it's in the brief of the
        Association of American Editorial
        Cartoonists -- that has George
        Washington being led on a donkey.
        And underneath there's a caption that
        the man leading the donkey is leading
        an ass...

                    JUSTICE SCALIA
        I can handle that. I think George
        could handle that.
                (a few CHUCKLES)
        But that's a far cry from committing
        incest with your mother in an
        outhouse.
                (a huge LAUGH from the room)
        I mean, there's no line between the
        two?

                    ISAACMAN
        No. There's no line, since what
        you're talking about is a matter of
        taste -- not law. That's the issue,
        because nobody literally believes
        that Jerry Falwell is being accused
        of committing incest --

                    JUSTICE MARSHALL
        So why did Hustler have him and his
        mother together??

                    ISAACMAN
          They had him and his mother together
          to show what's called in literary
          form "travesty." This is a man who
          is so self-righteous in the area of
          sex, telling everybody else what to
          do, telling them what to read, acting
          as though he has more knowledge than
          they do about how they live their
          lives. The ad might say that he is
          incestuous, but what it symbolically
          communicates is he's a hypocrite.

Larry silently agrees.

                    JUSTICE MARSHALL
          And what public purpose does that
          serve?

                    ISAACMAN
          It serves the same public purpose as
          having Garry Trudeau in "Doonesbury"
          call George Bush a wimp. It makes
          people look at Bush a little bit
          differently.
                    (building to his finale)
          Because, this is not just a dispute
          between Hustler and Jerry Falwell.
          This case affects everything that
          goes on in our national life. We
          have a long tradition of satiric
          commentary, and you can't pick up a
          newspaper in this country without
          seeing cartoons or editorials that
          have critical comments about people.
          And if Jerry Falwell can sue, so can
          any other public figure. Because if
          you say something critical about a
          person, it's going to cause emotional
          distress. We all know that. It's
          an easy thing to show, and that's why
          it's a meaningless standard.
                    (beat)
          All it does... is allow the
          punishment of unpopular speech.

Isaacman lets this idea hang, then sits down.

Larry is blown away. He smiles proudly at Isaacman.

The Justices nod.

                    CHIEF JUSTICE REHNQUIST
          Thank you, Mr. Isaacman.

                                        CUT TO:

199   EXT. U.S. SUPREME COURT - DAY   199

Pandemonium on the Court's steps. JOURNALISTS mob the exiting participants, circling in groups around Larry, Keating, and Falwell.

> REPORTER #1
> Reverend, are you confident that you will win the case?

> REV. FALWELL
> Absolutely! There's no way the Supreme Court will side with a sleaze merchant like Larry Flynt.

> REPORTER #2
> Mr. Keating, why are you here today?

> CHARLES KEATING
> To show my support for those who believe that pornography should be outlawed. This smut is the most dangerous menace to our country today! All decent citizens demand ACTION! They want pornography where it belongs -- IN JAIL!

Larry has the biggest crowd.

> REPORTER #3
> Larry, why'd you bother appealing? Why didn't you just pay the fine?

> LARRY
> Do you have to ask? We are talking about _freedom_!! Doesn't anybody know what that means anymore?! Doesn't anybody realize that if _I_ lose, then _you_ lose?!
> (his eyes are getting moist)
> I've been accused of hiding behind the First Amendment. Well, you're damn right I do! 'Cause I am the _worst_! But if the Constitution protects a crazy man like me... then it'll protect all Americans.

The reporters are silent. Larry is all choked up.

> REPORTER
> Do you have any regrets, Larry?

A long pause.

We slowly PUSH IN to Larry. His voice drops to a hush.

LARRY
Only one...

CUT TO:

200   EXT. FLYNT MANSION - DAY   200

The green estate sits silent, like a beautiful unused resort.

201   INT. MANSION - DAY   201

The big house is like a mausoleum. All the expensive antiques
are perfectly arranged and dusted clean... but there's no sign
of life. Room after room, empty.

Upstairs, every door is open. The camera slowly travels toward
Larry's bedroom... and inside, we faintly hear a WOMAN'S
GIGGLE. Oddly, it sounds like Althea...

We ENTER the room...

202   INT. BEDROOM   202

Larry is slumped in bed, remote control in hand, staring at the
TV.

ON THE TV is an old HOME MOVIE of Althea. She is happy,
healthy, vigorous, smiling...

Larry stares, teary-eyed. Suddenly, the phone RINGS. Larry
slowly answers it.

LARRY (on phone)
Yeah...

INTERCUT:

203   INT. SUPREME COURT CORRIDOR - DAY   203

Isaacman is on a pay phone. People stream past.

ISAACMAN (on phone)
Larry, the decision came down! Do
you want to hear it?

LARRY
Is it good or bad?

ISAACMAN
(toying)
It's unanimous. And the Chief
Justice wrote it himself.

LARRY
(losing patience)
But is that <u>good or bad</u>?

Pause.

                    ISAACMAN
          Let me read it to you.
                    (he holds up a sheaf of papers)
          "At the heart of the First Amendment
          is the recognition of the fundamental
          importance of the free flow of
          ideas... The freedom to speak one's
          mind is not only an aspect of
          individual liberty, but essential to
          the quest for truth and the vitality
          of society as a whole..."

Larry is looking pleased.

                    ISAACMAN
          "In the world of debate about public
          affairs, many things done with
          motives that are less than admirable
          are protected by the First
          Amendment... The fact that society
          may find speech offensive is not a
          sufficient reason to suppress it --"

                    LARRY
                    (interrupting)
          So we did it...?

Isaacman stops reading. Pause, then he smiles warmly.

                    ISAACMAN
          Yeah... we did it.

ANGLE - LARRY

His face lights up. He softly speaks.

                    LARRY
          Thanks, Alan.

Larry quietly hangs up. Then he turns to the TV.

ON THE TV - Young Althea dances sensuously, at night on the
lawn of the Columbus mansion. Light from the windows picks her
out of the darkness.

                    LARRY'S VOICE (on TV)
          Strip, baby!

Althea stops dancing. She looks directly at the camera.

                    ALTHEA (on TV)
          Why should I...?

                    LARRY'S VOICE (on TV)
          For posterity! When you're old and
          ugly, you'll love to look at this.

Althea grins. She resumes dancing... elegant... teasing...

                    ALTHEA (on TV)
      I'll never be old and ugly. <u>You</u>
      will...

She starts to strip...

CLOSEUP - LARRY

And he smiles sadly, very emotional, and very bittersweet.

                              FADE OUT.

THE END

CREDITS ROLL:

LARRY FLYNT LIVES IN LOS ANGELES AND PUBLISHES 29 MAGAZINES.
HE IS STILL CONFINED TO A WHEELCHAIR. HIS ASSAILANT WAS NEVER
BROUGHT TO JUSTICE.

JERRY FALWELL REMAINS ONE OF THE MOST RESPECTED RELIGIOUS
FIGURES IN AMERICA.

ALAN ISAACMAN LIVES IN LOS ANGELES AND IS STILL LARRY FLYNT'S
ATTORNEY.

CHARLES KEATING WAS CONVICTED ON 72 COUNTS OF RACKETEERING,
FRAUD, AND CONSPIRACY. HIS TRIAL REVEALED HIS ACTIONS COST
TAXPAYERS OVER 2 BILLION DOLLARS.

SCENE NOTES

BY SCOTT ALEXANDER & LARRY KARASZEWSKI

We will now attempt to explain the transition from what you have just read, to the final film. Moviemaking is a constantly evolving process, and ideas change for endless reasons. We did two official drafts by ourselves. Then we did two drafts with Milos. Then after location scouting in Memphis, we did another draft for arcane production needs (example: they couldn't find a suitable two-story mansion). Then on-set, the actors did some improvisation.

As of press time, the film is in postproduction...and things are still in flux. The first cut was three hours long. The most recent cut was two hours and nine minutes. Moral of the story? Don't fall in love with anything, because it's all up for grabs. Film is ultimately a director's medium, but when a hundred cast and crew members bump up against each other, unpredictable mitoses occur. The process can be brutal...or—exhilarating.

Sc. 1–3: These are basically unchanged, except we simplified the dialogue. This is particularly true in Sc. 3, where Milos thought there was too much talking. Now, Larry doesn't say much more than "I just want to make an honest buck."

During the Hillbilly moment, it's also interesting how Milos focused on the dollar bills and Larry's gaze—setting up his character for life.

Sc. 4: The bar fight and Jimmy's reaction were cut from the shooting script. Everything else was the same. But on-set...Milos reinterpreted the scene completely, without changing the words. The crowd is listless, not rocking, and Larry's delivery of his lines is bored. Woody played it distracted—a man looking for new excitement in his life.

Sc. 9: This is one of the most improvised scenes in the movie. Dozens of actresses read for the part of Althea, and they were given this scene, scene 40 (the marriage proposal), and scene 82 (Larry tells Althea he's born again). Milos felt Althea was a raw, ferocious character, and he encouraged spontaneity. From these sessions came hours of alternative versions.

Thus, when it was time for Courtney Love to play these three scenes in the movie, she used her audition versions. Milos wanted crazed realism between Woody and Courtney, so he utilized two cameras, letting them perform in real time. It's not exactly what we wrote, but it is vivid.

One minor note: The reference to her being "seventeen and a half" was cut from the shooting script. This was a matter of screenwriting de-emphasis. Courtney certainly isn't a teenager, though Hollywood has a fine tradition of thirty-year-olds playing high schoolers. But because the movie tracks fifteen years, we either needed a younger actress playing old, or an older actress playing young. Once the choice was made, we pulled out specific problem lines—so we wouldn't point a flashing arrow at it.

Sc. 10, 12: The dialogue got cut.

Sc. 14: We put Althea's back story in this scene. During production, Milos moved it to Sc. 82.

Sc. 15: This was shot but deleted. By opening Sc. 16 with Larry reading *Playboy,* the transition wasn't needed.

Sc. 16: Chester's cartooning moment was cut—but this goes to a larger change. The delineation between his cartoonist character and Arlo's sardonic editor was eliminated. Instead, three actors became general staffers Arlo, Chester, and Miles.

The reference to "Alan Jay Lerner" became "Buckminster Fuller"—we had to use a celebrity who had done a real *Playboy* interview.

Sc. 17: Larry deciding to start a magazine got changed to Larry showing off newly rented offices. But then Milos dropped it during editing. The audience knows going in that Larry created *Hustler.* The quicker we get there, the better.

Sc. 19: This scene is a perfect example of Milos's naturalism at play. We had one line of atmosphere dialogue: "Do we type the numbers on the pages, or will the printer do it for us?" This moment became the launching pad for thirty seconds of ad-libbed staffer silliness.

Sc. 20: This scene is our parody of a biopic's traditional "lightbulb-over-the-head" moment. Perhaps Larry never had the sudden epiphany of how to photograph a woman's genitals—but he should have. It's like when Don Ameche invented the telephone.

Sc. 21: This was cut from the shooting script. It was cute, but unnecessary.

Sc. 24: Milos, Woody, and Courtney added substantial improv here. Our scene was about Larry blaming himself—they made it Larry and Althea turning on each other.

Sc. 27–28: Scene 28 was cut in script stage. The subway scene was supposed to be shot—but kept getting pushed, pushed, pushed down the schedule. Finally, it was eliminated. This was a perfect lesson in screenwriting reality: If you have a ten-second scene in an expensive location with lots of extras and it's all expendable … chances are it won't get shot.

Sc. 30: This is an example of how scenes evolve over time. Our final shooting script has Charles Keating in a hotel banquet room, lecturing to proper middle-class people.

Our original version was much odder and more mysterioso. Keating and his uptight buddies were gathered in a dark office, brooding worriedly. They pass around *Hustler* in a hermetically sealed plastic bag. Then they fret that *Oh, Calcutta!* is coming through town. This approach was funny, but too removed.

Sc. 31: In our early drafts, we had Larry at the adding machine and Althea sleeping. But we realized the script was shortchanging her contributions to the magazine. So we added many little moments of her taking action. Hopefully, these tweaks add up to something.

Sc. 37: The basement scene got shot, but cut. This one hurt. It turned out terrific—the actors playing the parents were very touching. But the film was simply too long.

Sc. 40: The scripted lines pretty much got thrown out the window. Woody and Courtney basically said the dialogue they had worked out during her auditions.

Sc. 44: This scene was cut in half during editing. It's an example of "preachifying"… piling on bombast and exposition. Making the First Amendment argument was very important to us—but information that seems essential on the page can become tedious on the screen. A drop of background goes a long way.

As a side note, we've enclosed an alternate sequence from our first draft. This section included a subplot culled from Larry's wacky life—terrorizing the citizens of Ohio with Vietnam gore. We cut it because the script was too long. However, the juxtaposition of sex and graphic violence was a good idea … so we moved it to the rally scene.


```
INT. MANSION - DAY


Larry marches furiously around the huge living room,
screaming in a tirade. Althea and Arlo calmly watch.


                    LARRY
          I CAN'T BELIEVE IT! How can our coun-
          try do this?!
```

                    ARLO
        Larry, it ain't nothin' new. The
        fuckin' post office burned <u>Ulysses</u>.

                    ALTHEA
        Hmm...didn't hear about that.
                (beat)
        All I know is twenty-five years
        seems like an awful long time. My
        cousin Bobby shot a preacher, and
        he only got seven!

                    ARLO
                (sarcastic)
        Well your cousin Bobby only hurt
        one person. Larry is polluting the
        minds of millions.

                    LARRY
        Oh, that's real funny! See, that's
        exactly how these morons think. They
        got their priorities all fucked up!
                (livid)
        Violence is okay, but sex ain't!

They all mull this over. Finally —

                    ARLO
        Have you ever noticed that sex is
        legal, but you can't show pictures
        of it — yet murder is illegal, and
        you <u>can</u> show pictures of it??

                    ALTHEA
        That's weird.

                    LARRY
        It's fucked up! It's all fucked up!

                    ALTHEA
        During Vietnam, they showed dead
        bodies on the TV every night....

                              ARLO
                    Now that's obscene.

CLOSEUP - LARRY
Hmm! He suddenly gets a wicked gleam in his eye....

                                             CUT TO:

INT. PRINTING PLANT - DAY

Printing presses WHIR. Bright red paper rushes by in a
blur.

                                             CUT TO:

EXT. CINCINNATI SUBURB - DAY

A postal truck drives along. At each house, the MAILMAN
inserts a bundle of mail wrapped in a bright red brochure.

At the closest mailbox, a SWEET OLD LADY exits her
cute little house and shuffles toward us. She takes
her mail and casually examines it. Some bills, a nice
Pennysaver with coupons, and then — the brochure.

In bold lettering, it says "THE REAL OBSCENITY: WAR."
Underneath is a horrific PHOTO of a soldier with his
head blown off.

The old lady gasps and tumbles back.

                         SWEET OLD LADY
                    Oh dear Jesus and Mary!

                                             CUT TO:

INT. LARRY'S OFFICE - DAY
Isaacman is frantically yelling at Larry.

                           ISAACMAN
                    How many of these brochures went
                    out?!!

                               151

                              LARRY
                          (nonchalant)
                400,000.

                            ISAACMAN
            "400,000"??? What were you thinking?!

                              LARRY
            It's every household in Cincinnati.
            I thought it would help.

                            ISAACMAN
            What — everyone opening their
            mailbox and gagging?! Look, leave
            the defense strategy to me!

     Isaacman stops hyperventilating. He lowers his voice.

                            ISAACMAN
            I understand you're upset, but we
            have to go about this in a smarter,
            classier way.

Sc. 45-48: The *60 Minutes/New York Times* section was yanked right before shooting. We thought it was important to explain Larry's education—his transition from hillbilly to eloquent speaker. So we showed him learning about the issues (and pulled his lines from real interviews). But Milos felt this area slowed down the movie, so it got cut.

As a side note, Milos took all the *60 Minutes* dialogue and moved it to Scene 70—Larry being released from the Georgia jail. This was shot. But then, in editing, most of it got cut out again, because it slowed down the movie!

Sc. 49: A funny production story: This scene depicts an angry crowd protesting Larry's court appearance. While we were filming the extras, a Memphis TV crew showed up. That night on the news, they ran a story...claiming this angry crowd was protesting our movie! A beautiful example of the media reporting what they want to report.

Sc. 50-53: As a rule, all courtroom scenes are based on transcripts and articles from the period. We used as much real dialogue as we could, but with massive editing. Leis's cross-examination of Larry is different, though— it's an interweaving of statements both men made over the years, but not to each other.

In the film, Milos added a coda where Larry discusses the dirty Santa Claus picture.

Sc. 54: This was the last scene cut out, right before the film got locked. During a test screening, many audience members were confused about how Larry gets out of jail. The dialogue here only exacerbated the problem.

Sc. 55: The verdict scene is a good example of how movies are reflections of the time they're made in. While we were doing script revisions, the O.J. trial was consuming America, and Milos was one of its biggest fans.

In the scene, we were content to say "Guilty" and move on. But Milos felt that in an era of O.J., the public now wanted, and craved, courtroom procedure. So he added all the back-and-forth of reality, to drag out the tension....."Mr. Foreman, have you arrived at a verdict? Will the defendant please stand and face the jury? Please hand the verdict to the bailiff...."

In a hilarious postscript, Milos asked the real Larry Flynt to have a cameo. Larry was unsure—so Milos suggested the part of the judge, because he only has a few lines. Larry agreed. But then Milos turned around and gave the judge an extra page of dialogue!

Sc. 56: This scene as shot is an exact recreation of an old piece of Ohio TV newsfilm.

Sc. 57–59: On-set, Milos substantially reworked this sequence. He eliminated Ma Flynt and made it a tender love scene between Larry and Althea.

Sc. 60: This published version of the script includes Dick Gregory, who subsequently got completely cut out. We liked having him in the movie, because he represented a type of person that Larry befriended—the radical politicized celebrity: Dick Gregory, Timothy Leary, Frank Zappa, Dennis Hopper, Terry Southern...each was his buddy at various times. Larry threw money at their various causes, and in return, they enlightened him with their Left Wing ideas. Most of them even contributed articles to *Hustler*.

In a biopic, you don't have time for every person or place your character ever experienced. So when a single individual or idea can stand in for many, you embrace it. "Dick Gregory" is not a composite character, but he does express sentiments that many of these different men did. Unfortunately, we had to cut him out when we shortened the script. So we gave many of his lines to Arlo, making Arlo the savvy educator. But then Milos split those lines among all the staffers. The net result is that Larry appears to teach himself.

P.S. At the real Cincinnati rally, Rod McKuen and F. Lee Bailey made appearances.

Sc. 61–63: This was all shot, then cut. We thought it was critical to show the magazine becoming political...but the editing room disagreed.

The person we really feel sorry for is our loyal associate producer George Linardos, who spent weeks in the bowels of *Hustler*'s photo archives. He almost drove himself mad, tracking down original artwork and negatives that hadn't seen daylight since the '70s. We assumed they would be quite prominent in the movie. But ultimately, they're just background.

Sc. 64: All the talk about Althea posing was cut—instead, we just see her pose. We sometimes forget that film's a visual medium. You don't always need the yapping.

Sc. 65: We wanted Larry's plane to be pink. Unfortunately for us, Larry Flynt offered his current plane to the production free of charge. That plane is black. It's hard to argue for the color of a prop, when it saves the movie a hunk of money.

Sc. 66-69: The reporters' scene was moved to the book shop. Another screen-writing lesson: If a production manager can have two short scenes in a bookshop and a plane, or one long scene in the bookshop... he'll always choose the latter.

Sc. 75-81: None of this made it to the shooting script. This born-again sequence was our biggest disagreement with Milos. We thought it was great and raised the movie to brilliant heights of surrealism. The Jesus/Paul/Lenny Bruce scene even got excerpted in *Time* magazine.

But Milos didn't like it. He had two principal reasons: One, he is a naturalistic filmmaker and wasn't into effects and fantasy. And two, he argued that when the average person has a born-again experience, it isn't lightning, music, and chatty ghosts. It's quiet. Personal.

Desperate, we tried swaying Milos by pointing out that the airplane scene was Larry's version of the event. Also, it connected to the last scene in our original draft:

```
Larry is choked up. A reporter shouts out.

                    REPORTER
          So Larry, have you achieved
          everything you wanted?

A long pause.

We slowly PUSH IN to Larry. A sad smile comes over him,
and then he speaks in a low, sincere whisper.

                    LARRY
          Almost.
                    (beat)
          I just wish Althea could've been
          here to see this.

EXT. HEAVEN - DAY

Up on a fluffy white cloud, Jesus, Paul, and Lenny
Bruce look down.

Then Althea floats over and joins them. She stares
down at Larry, then smiles.

                                        FADE OUT.


            THE END
```

We thought it was cool. Milos's response? Dump it. Let's come up with something simple. So the three of us went through a dozen conversion scenes: Larry and Althea have sex on the plane—and he becomes obsessed with the perfection of birds. Or the plane almost crashes—and on the tarmac, Larry finds God. Or the plane lands fine—and cinematographer Philippe Rousselot shoots a sunrise so astonishingly beautiful that we essentially see God.

In the final film, there's just a bird…then a plane…and then the scene ends! That's it. The approach works fine, but it's light-years from our original intention.

Sc. 84–88: All these scenes were cut. Only the Keating scene was shot.

Sc. 89: Dick Gregory got eliminated from this scene. It's hard to defend—he had nothing to do with it. But we wanted to keep his "juice subplot"…he introduces Larry to an all-juice diet, and then that saves Larry's life after the gunshots. It was intriguing irony, but expendable.

Sc. 90: Milos only used the top of the church scene. He discovered a local Memphis choir and fell in love with them—so their music became the focus of the scene.

Sc. 91: This got cut from the shooting script. Now the magazine shows up in Sc. 92. If you can do two locations as one...

Sc. 95: Isaacman's speech was shot, but cut. Similar ideas show up in his Supreme Court speech.

Sc. 97: After Larry gets shot, Milos added a nice spooky touch: the gunman calmly walking away.

Sc. 100–102: This was all filmed, then cut. Instead of neat transitions, the sequence is an acceleration of frantic disorder.

Sc. 103: We cut out the doctor talking about juice. It was quite interesting, but sometimes research plays more like fun facts than drama.

Sc. 104: This scene was shot as is, but in the final cut, all you hear is Althea telling Larry he's paralyzed. Our instinct as writers is to always throw a few weird curveballs before important moments. But in editing, scenes often get distilled down to their essence.

Sc. 105–106: The nonsense with the doctor and the photographer got cut from the shooting script. We liked it, because it happened—Larry's wounds actually showed up in *Hustler.* In the film, Ruth simply enters Sc. 104.

Sc. 108: This got cut.

Sc. 111: In our earlier drafts, Larry always planned on moving to L.A. He purchases Sonny Bono's house as a prelude to greatness. But then when he's shot, the dream turns sour: The new house has a wall of steps…it's not wheelchair accessible.

Milos felt this was probably too busy. So now, L.A. is played as a sudden idea: Let's move to a place where perverts are welcome. Incidentally, the house used in the film was actually Larry's at one time.

Sc. 115: This was our elegant solution to an interesting structural problem: Larry Flynt fell into a five-year haze of drugs and surgeries after his shooting. He stopped running the magazine. He lost interest in life. He ceased being an interesting movie protagonist. Yet, this period was smack in the middle of our story. We couldn't ignore it.

So we made five years passing almost a sick blackout joke. Instead of hiding it, we played it up—the door literally shuts for five years. Then Milos joined in the absurdity by adding an on-screen counter.

Sc. 116: The disturbing top of the scene, with Larry and Althea, was cut from the shooting script. Also, Milos played the doctor much more somber and awkward than we did.

Sc. 122-129: These are all cut. Larry created chaos on a massive scale, and we wanted to show the scope. But none of these got filmed. Sc. 123-128 were actually in the shooting script...but there's always a few scenes in any movie that get sacrificed to last-minute problems (weather, budget, scheduling, etc).

In our first draft, we had even more chaos. When Korean Airliner 007 got shot down, Georgia Congressman Larry McDonald was aboard. Larry Flynt obsessed this into a massive right-wing conspiracy. It culminated with *Hustler* publishing naked pictures of the dead congressman with a 300-pound hooker.

Sc. 130: When Larry obtained the DeLorean tapes, in real life he gave them to a famous television news producer whose name became the character's name. But then the Columbia lawyers called—we couldn't depict a respected journalist running around in his pajamas. We had to choose—call him by his real name ... or show pj's. We can never resist a cheap joke, so pj's won out.

Sc. 133: The Judge Mantke scenes are based upon court cases with two different L.A. judges: Robert Takasugi and Manuel Real. Because we combined the trials, we changed the name.

The role ended up being played by D'Army Bailey, a real Memphis judge who suddenly found himself starring in a movie.

Sc. 134-135: These got cut. Stopping and restarting the DeLorean trial was too convoluted.

Sc. 136-139: Larry running for president was all shot, then cut out. We loved the epic quality it brought. But in editing, Milos decided the trial was symbolism enough for Larry's screwing it to America.

In our original draft, we went even further with the candidacy. We included Larry selecting his running mate....

EXT. BOWLING ALLEY - NIGHT

A SEXY LADY TV REPORTER does a stand-up in front of the
bowling alley.

> SEXY REPORTER
> ...tapping into the anger and
> frustration that working people have
> toward Washington and politicians.
> At this rate, Larry Flynt should
> have little trouble getting his
> supporters into the voting booth
> next fall. The only question is,
> what will they do there?
> (smirk)
> This is Bonnie Brown, Channel 3 News.

She lowers her mike. The CAMERAMAN turns off his light.
Suddenly, punked-out Althea shimmies out of the
shadows. She seductively leans in to the woman.

> ALTHEA
> Hey Cutie, do you like to party?

EST. ROADSIDE HOTEL - NIGHT

INT. HOTEL ROOM - NIGHT

Althea and the sexy reporter are naked. The woman blushes.

> SEXY REPORTER
> I can't believe this...you are so
> kinky....

Althea gives her a long, deep kiss.

> ALTHEA
> C'mon...Larry will love it.

The woman finally nods. So Althea hands her a rubber

George Bush mask. Althea pulls on a Reagan mask.

INT. HOTEL BEDROOM - NIGHT

The naked "Reagan" is humping the naked "Bush" on the bed.

Larry sits to the side, shouting out orders. He's
wearing an admiral's hat.

> LARRY
> C'mon, screw it to Bush! Harder!
> Show him what it's like to be on
> the bottom of the ticket!

Suddenly "Bush" looks over.

> REPORTER (MUFFLED IN MASK)
> Hey Larry, that reminds me. Have you
> picked your V.P.?

Larry gets a quizzical expression. He thinks....

>   CUT TO:

EST. PINE RIDGE RESERVATION - DAY

A poor Indian reservation. Small log homes sit on the
land. Suddenly the pink plane ROARS overhead.

INT. LOG HOME - DAY

Isaacman rolls Larry into a meeting room of INDIANS.
RUSSELL MEANS, a large, serious Indian with black
braided hair, stands up.

> ISAACMAN
> (not quite sure why he's here)
> Uh, Larry Flynt, I'd like you to
> meet Russell Means, leader of the
> American Indian Movement.

Larry and Russell shake.

> RUSSELL MEANS
> So you're looking for a running mate?

                              LARRY
              Join with me. I'm the candidate for
              the oppressed and exploited. I'll
              give you political attention on a
              national level — you can tell everyone
              about your 371 broken treaties.

                          RUSSELL MEANS
                           (intrigued)
              Hmm. An Indian has never had that
              kind of forum before....

Isaacman pipes up.

                            ISAACMAN
              Yeah, I can't wait to see you at
              the debates wiping the floor with
              Sam Donaldson.

Sc. 141: In the shooting script, we changed this scene to Isaacman calling Larry. In the film, the trial never stops. The court demands to know the source of the tape, and Larry refuses. This leads to Sc. 144.

Sc. 142–143: The bogus audiotape sequence was cut a week before shooting. We thought it was really funny…but it seemed to create endless confusion among readers of the script. It was one "tape discussion" too many. Also, as surrounding scenes got trimmed, they made the remaining DeLorean section too prominent.

Sc. 150, 151, 153: These scenes got cut out. Short transition scenes rarely survive the editing room.

Sc. 156–159: None of these scenes were shot. The "First Lady" discussion got moved to a campaigning scene, but then was cut in editing.

Sc. 161–163: These never made it to the shooting script. We initially included the Alaska episode because it made us laugh. It typified the sort of rebellious performance theater Larry was creating at that time. But ultimately, it was an obvious cut.

Sc. 170: We thought the blizzard of terrible words was hilarious. It was a way to let the audience figure out the content of the ad, by context. If we had actually shown the ad, it might have gotten us an NC–17.

Milos said it was an interesting idea…for a different director. It didn't jibe with his naturalistic approach. So we cut it.

Sc. 175: This scene was shot in Larry Flynt's actual office.

Sc. 176: This scene was an example of script development improving a film. It wasn't in our initial drafts. But everybody was bothered that Althea fell out of the third act. So, as a structurally perfunctory solution, we added her re-hiring Isaacman.

Oddly enough, the finished scene turned out terrific. It's one of Courtney Love and Edward Norton's best moments.

Sc. 179: This was one of the only reordered scenes. In the final cut, it precedes the Supreme Court.

Sc. 182: Our version of the scene closely followed the court transcript. But on location, Milos and Edward reworked it into Isaacman cross-examining Falwell. Their version explicitly explains the illogic of the libel claim.

If you find the Falwell case interesting, there's an excellent law book analyzing its intricacies—*Jerry Falwell v. Larry Flynt,* by Rodney Smolla. It covers more background and issues than we could ever fit into thirty minutes of a movie.

Sc. 184-185: These are cut.

Sc. 188-190: These scenes got cut. As a nonsensical side note, when Larry leaves prison, we originally had fellow psycho-ward inmate John Hinckley waving good-bye.

Sometimes, you can do too much research.

Sc. 199-203: We reworked the last three pages many, many times. The problem was that the film had numerous story strands: The love story. The legal story. Larry's redemption. Larry's rags to riches. And Larry's bittersweet resolution—success tempered with tragedy.

We had to figure out how to bring it all together. Everything had to tie up, yet be satisfying dramatically. In various drafts, we tried, then discarded, many ideas: Larry and Isaacman wait in the law office while the decision comes over a fax. Or Rehnquist writes out his decision in longhand, and we follow the suspenseful process—it gets typed, xeroxed, distributed. Or we reconvene at the Court, and Rehnquist dramatically delivers the decision. Or we watch Falwell get the verdict, and we relish in his defeat.

But ultimately...none of this mattered. Working with Milos, we arrived at a simple, poignant ending. Larry lies alone in bed—while Althea flickers on the TV, and Isaacman calls on the phone. It brought everything full circle: He has his wealth. He has his decision. He has his place in history. But...he doesn't have his true love. At the end of the day, the victories are hollow, and he'll only have his memories to live with.

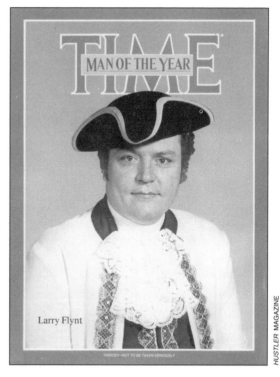

Left: Woody Harrelson as Larry Flynt.
Right: The real Larry Flynt in a *Hustler* parody of a *Time* magazine cover.

ALTHEA

A MAN SHOULD HAVE HIS
CAKE AND EAT IT, TOO.

49

Opposite: Althea Leasure poses for *Hustler* Magazine.
Above: Courtney Love plays Althea Leasure.
Below left: Portrait of Courtney Love as Althea.
Below right: Portrait of Althea.

164

Opposite above: Larry (*Woody Harrelson*) and Althea (*Courtney Love*) on their wedding day.

Opposite below: The real Larry and Althea on their wedding day with Larry's brother Jimmy (on left).

Right: Larry and Jimmy Flynt.

Below: Brett Harrelson as Jimmy Flynt.

COURTESY LARRY FLYNT

Above left: The real Jerry Falwell.
Above right: The real Charles Keating.
Below: Charles Keating (*James Cromwell*) and Jerry Falwell (*Richard Paul*).

Above left: Edward Norton as Alan Isaacman.
Above right: The real Alan Isaacman.
Below: Milos Forman directing James Carville as Simon Leis.

Above: The real Larry Flynt makes his screen debut as a judge.
Below: The press bombard Althea (*Courtney Love*) and Jimmy
(*Brett Harrelson*) outside the Cincinnati courthouse.

Above left: Donna Hanover plays Ruth Carter Stapleton.
Above right: The real Ruth Carter Stapleton.
Below: Ruth (*Donna Hanover*) baptizes Larry (*Woody Harrelson*).

LARRY FLYNT: AMERICAN DISSIDENT

Dissident writers and artists in the Soviet Union and other nations are being vilified and imprisoned, and President Jimmy Carter has stated his deep concern. In the wake of recent events, we urge the president to take a closer look at the restrictions of freedom of expression in America itself.

In Cincinnati, Ohio, publisher Larry Flynt was convicted of using *Hustler* magazine to pander obscenity and of engaging in organized crime. Ohio law states that engaging in organized crime is five or more persons conspiring to commit a crime. Mr. Flynt was accused of working with members of his staff to produce *Hustler*—a charge such as this could easily be leveled at any publisher in the country. This clearly amounts to government harassment of a dissident publication.

As a result, Flynt was immediately sentenced to 7 to 25 years in prison and was fined a total of $11,000. Bond was originally refused, pending appeal—an obvious infringement of his rights.

We the undersigned wish to protest the infringement of Mr. Flynt's rights under the First Amendment because it is a threat to the rights of all Americans. We cannot, under any circumstances, approve of government censorship. Further, we urge President Carter and all our fellow citizens to strengthen their commitment to protecting every American's right to freedom of expression.

Woody Allen	John Dean	Gerald Green	Arthur Kretchmer	Eric Norden	Peter Stone
Michael Arlen	Joan Didion	Dan Greenburg	Jonathan Z. Larsen	Eleanor Perry	Gay Talese
Joe Armstrong	Digby Diehl	David Halberstam	Nat Lehrman	Gerard Piel	Nan Talese
Chuck Ashman	Larry DuBois	Pete Hamill	John Leonard	Nicholas Pileggi	Gore Vidal
Noel Behn	John G. Dunn	Joe Hanson	Jay Levin	Dotson Rader	Nicholas Von
Arthur Bell	Daniel Ellsberg	Hugh Hefner	Thomas H. Lipscomb	Rex Reed	Hoffman
Ronnie Bennett	Stanley Fleishman	Joseph Heller	Marshall Lumsden	Richard Rhodes	Irving Wallace
Warren Boroson	Bruce Jay Friedman	Tony Hendra	J. Anthony Lukas	Harold Robbins	George T. Wein
Malcolm Brady	Judge Charles Galbreath	Warren Hinckle	Peter Maas	Ned Rorem	Jann Wenner
Barbara Cady	Brendan Gill	George A. Hirsch	Norman Mailer	Richard Rosenzweig	Clark Whelton
Vincent Canby	Allen Ginsberg	A. E. Hotchner	Bill Manville	Barney Rosset	Bruce Williamson
Robert Christgau	Ralph Ginzburg	Peter Kleinman	Milt Machlin	Mike Royko	Emanuel L. Wolf
Ramsey Clark	Herb Gold	Arthur Knight	Rudy Maxa	Mike Salisbury	Robert Yoakum
Harry Crews	Al Goldstein	Michael Kramer	Frederic Morton	Robert Sherrill	Sol Yurick
Judith Crist	Jim Goode	Paul Krassner	Philip Nobile	Geoffrey Stokes	Mark Zussman

Sponsored by
AMERICANS FOR A FREE PRESS

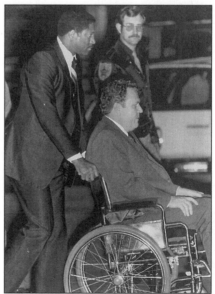

Opposite: Flynt's Americans for a Free Press full-page ad, as it appeared
in *The New York Times*, February 20, 1977.
Above: Larry Flynt speaks to the press.
Below left: Larry (*Woody Harrelson*) and Althea (*Courtney Love*) outside the L.A. mansion.
Below right: Larry Flynt on his way to testify in the lawsuit filed against him by Jerry Falwell.

Jerry Falwell talks about his first time.*

FALWELL: My first time was in an outhouse outside Lynchburg, Virginia.

INTERVIEWER: Wasn't it a little cramped?

FALWELL: Not after I kicked the goat out.

INTERVIEWER: I see. You must tell me all about it.

FALWELL: I never *really* expected to make it with Mom, but then after she showed all the other guys in town such a good time, I figured, "What the hell!"

INTERVIEWER: But your mom? Isn't that a bit odd?

FALWELL: I don't think so. Looks don't mean that much to me in a woman.

INTERVIEWER: Go on.

FALWELL: Well, we were drunk off our God-fearing asses on Campari, ginger ale and soda—that's called a Fire and Brimstone—at the time. And Mom looked better than a Baptist whore with a $100 donation.

INTERVIEWER: Campari in the crapper with Mom . . . how interesting. Well, how was it?

FALWELL: The Campari was great, but Mom passed out before I could come.

INTERVIEWER: Did you ever try it again?

FALWELL: Sure . . .

lots of times. But not in the outhouse. Between Mom and the shit, the flies were too much to bear.

INTERVIEWER: We meant the Campari.

FALWELL: Oh, yeah. I always get sloshed before I go out to the pulpit. You don't think I could lay down all that bullshit *sober*, do you?

© 1983—Imported by Campari U.S.A. New York, NY 48°proof Spirit Aperitif (Liqueur)

Campari, like all liquor, was made to mix you up. It's a light, 48-proof, refreshing spirit, just mild enough to make you drink too much before you know you're schnockered. For your first time, mix it with orange juice. Or maybe some white wine. Then you won't remember anything the next morning. **Campari. The mixable that smarts.**

CAMPARI You'll never forget your first time.

*AD PARODY—NOT TO BE TAKEN SERIOUSLY

HUSTLER MAGAZINE

HUSTLER MAGAZINE

Far left: Hustler magazines of the '70s.
Above: Campari ad parody of Falwell's "first time" in *Hustler* magazine (November 1983).

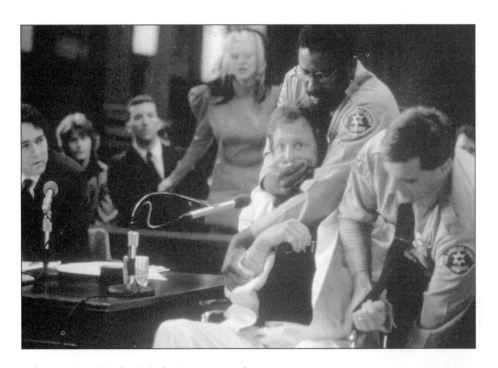

Above: Larry (*Woody Harrelson*) gets gagged.
Below: Isaacman (*Edward Norton*) and Larry (*Woody Harrelson*) in court.

Flynt (*Woody Harrelson*) at Althea's funeral.

AFTERWORD

TALKING WITH MILOS FORMAN
BY ADAM DAVIDSON

orn in 1932 in Čáslav, Czechoslovakia, near Prague, Milos
Forman was orphaned at the age
of eight after losing both his parents to
the Nazis in concentration camps. After
becoming interested in theater as a
young student, he eventually enrolled
in the University of Prague's Film
Institute. He began his feature film
career in 1963 with *Black Peter* and
subsequently gained international
attention with *Loves of a Blonde* (1965)
and *Fireman's Ball* (1967). After the
Soviet invasion, he emigrated to the
United States in 1968, making his first
American film three years later. *Taking
Off* starred Buck Henry and was written by Henry, Forman, and John
Guare. A string of exceptional films
followed—two winning Academy
Awards® for Best Director and Best
Picture, *One Flew Over the Cuckoo's Nest*
(1975) and *Amadeus* (1984). The oth-
ers were: a segment in *Visions of Eight*

(1973), a documentary about the 1972
Munich Olympics; and the feature
films *Hair* (1979), *Ragtime* (1981), and
Valmont (1989). Though they range in
size and scope, all are very personal
films and reflect Milos's unique combination of sensibilities: humor,
humanity, and substance.

The People vs. Larry Flynt marks Milos's
return to directing after seven years. It's
no surprise that he would be drawn personally to a film about censorship, as he
was witness to the Nazi and Soviet
occupation of Czechoslovakia, where
freedom of speech was practically eliminated. We first met in 1991. Even then,
censorship became an issue in the can-
cellation of a film we worked on
together involving Americans in Japan.
On the eve of the premiere of *The
People vs. Larry Flynt* before the presti-
gious New York Film Festival, Milos
and I spoke about the new film, free
speech, and American citizenship.

In the spirit of free speech, what would you like to say first?

First, I wanted to pay a compliment to the writers, because this was the kind of script directors dream about.

Why's that?

It had a strong, strong story; very interesting characters; a good structure; and it was so true to life that it opened itself to outside input.

What do you mean by outside input?

For example, that doesn't happen with, let's say, a Neil Simon script. Every line in it would be contrived in such a manner as to fit into the other lines. If you change one line, everything falls apart. But this script was so wonderful in that it opened itself, as a matter of fact, like a sponge, sucking in everything and allowing everyone from actors, to myself, even the police—whoever—to contribute.

And why does that make for a better movie?

I wouldn't say better but more interesting, because it creates the opportunity to get on-screen *unrepeatable* moments which, for me, is the spice of every film, as opposed to the theater where you know everything is rehearsed and usually feels that way.

You usually have an interesting story attached to the material you do. Tell me the history of this one.

I was getting about ten scripts every week for the last several years since the aborted project we had together. I got involved with one [*Disclosure*] for about six months but, again, that one didn't materialize for me. So for over a year I was just sitting reading scripts. I always try to read at least twenty-five pages of every script and, if it doesn't grab me by then, that's it. With this one, however, I opened it, read the title, and closed it immediately. I didn't read it at all.

How come?

Because I read the name "Larry Flynt" and my only knowledge, or notion, about him was as a sleaze and a pornographer. I was sure the script was another kind of exploitation movie. Only when Mr. Lantz [agent Robert Lantz] called to ask if I had read it did he tell me I should, as a courtesy to Oliver Stone. I didn't know it was an Oliver Stone production because on the cover it said Ixtlan Productions. I didn't know what Ixtlan was. So I read it right away as a courtesy to Oliver (people like Oliver Stone, you don't let them wait), and when I read it I immediately said, "Yes, I want to make this movie." Then something unusual in Hollywood happened. Within just a few days, Lisa Henson of Columbia Pictures flew to New York with the writers to meet me. We found out that we all had, if not identical, very similar opinions about how the film should be made.

Which were?

Well, that neither Larry Flynt nor his opposition would be the heroes. That the hero would be the Supreme Court of the United States, and everybody else would be simply human, with all their pros and all their cons. Also, that I was not going to glamorize pornography, because I am conditioned from my childhood to see pornography as *bad,* and I still feel that way. I feel intimidated when I have to look at these kinds of pictures.

You mean you feel embarrassed?

It embarrasses me if somebody sees me! I have this kind of education typical of puritanical Protestant families where, if you are caught looking at these kinds of magazines, you feel deeply embarrassed and you want to commit suicide, but yet when nobody's around you'd love to look at them, you know? Still, I have never bought *Hustler* magazine in my life.

But you knew about it, of course?

Of course I knew about it, but I didn't know anything about Larry Flynt.

That you learned from reading the script?

When I read it, I was absolutely fascinated with the life I discovered behind this dirty word, "Flynt." I made some phone calls to see if it was true, and as I found out, *everything* was true.

Once you agreed to make the movie, what was the next step?

Everything went so fast, which is unusual in Hollywood. First, I did my homework and brought to the authors a suggestion on how to cut the material down to a reasonable length.

Was that your only concern? A long script seems normal for a biopic—Gandhi, Lawrence of Arabia—*full lives don't fit easily into two hours.*

Scott and Larry did an incredible job structuring and sifting through *all* the events in Larry Flynt's life and then condensing it into a story that was acceptable as a film drama. It's not only normal to have a long script at first, it's better. Every scene was over-written, which is fine because it gives you something to work with. And though it was long, it still went pretty fast.

I know from our experience working together that you liked to sit in a room, and we'd talk and act out the scenes. But that was for a screenplay written from scratch. How does that process work in a script that has already been written?

I did it myself. The writers came to New York and we did some talking out loud together, but we didn't go through the painstaking process—the details of acting out every scene. I was doing that just by myself; later on we did that—but just for the final versions of the script.

What did you find connected you personally to the material?

The basic kick for me was that twice in my life I had experienced political regimes in which crusades against pornographers—perverts as they were called—turned into the worst censorship, where freedom of speech was practically eliminated entirely. Both the Nazis and the Communists started their regimes with crusades against perverts. I witnessed that, and not only did nobody oppose the oppressions, everybody applauded them, because who wants perverts to run free in the streets, right? Of course, then, when power was seized, they started to formulate laws against perverts. These laws were always formulated conveniently so that, when they wanted, they could brand anybody a pervert who didn't agree with their government. So it started with homosexuals and pornographers, and Jews and blacks, and finally you found out that Jesus Christ is a pervert, Shakespeare is a pervert, and William Faulkner is a pervert. Next, your plumber is a pervert. And finally, you know, you are a pervert.

What I love about this story is the journey Larry Flynt takes. It seems that many native-born Americans are not always appreciative of the freedoms and liberties we have. It's not necessarily out of indifference; it's simply from the privilege of having them since birth—we take them for granted. To me, this story is about an American becoming an "American," a politically cognizant citizen.

I'll tell you, this country is, when it comes to freedoms, the greatest country in the world: not by the will of its politicians but because this country is *condemned* to freedom by the diversity of its population—its races, religions, and philosophies. But the fact that it is the freest country in the world doesn't mean you can take it for granted, because we will never conquer the stupidity of fanatics and power-hungry megalomaniacs. We will never win over them. At the same time, we cannot afford to stop fighting them, for they can and will win over us. That's why we shouldn't take all these freedoms for granted, like something that is undeniably ours. Look, the Czechs thought the same way about their freedom, too, in the 1930s and were quickly in for a shock. The Germans were certainly not an undeveloped nation. It was the country of Goethe and Mozart. Suddenly, Hitler comes, and there was not enough opposition, not enough freedom fighters; and look what happened. So, obviously, it could happen anywhere.

What do you think really motivates Larry Flynt to fight for freedom?

I'm sure, at the beginning, what motivated Larry was not freedom. It was to make money and to meet girls. But because, suddenly, he finds that society is interfering with his lusts, his desires, he starts to fight it. And what he discovers is that what he is fighting is much bigger than him. Despite that, he doesn't buckle. That's what I admire most about him: that he didn't buckle; that he found out he was fighting a much bigger colossus than he was, but instead of trying to compromise or trying to accommodate, he grew to the size of the colossus to fight it.

It seems an unlikely fight for the Hugh Hefner and Bob Guccione types.

You know, in all honesty, I never expected to like Larry Flynt as a person. I admired his life, but I never expected to actually like him. But I must tell you, I kind of like him—a lot. Because he is absolutely unpretentious. You know with whom you are dealing. You can take everything he says for what it is. And he doesn't try to say he's anything other than what he is.

When did you and he first meet?

About a year ago—September. The production didn't have a green light but that was the first thing I had requested, to meet Larry Flynt—and Alan Isaacman—the real people, just to have a feeling. Larry Flynt was not in very good shape, but he was trying, trying hard to communicate.

Then when he got the script, the final version, I had a script conference with him. I was absolutely amazed. The day before, I had a script conference with Columbia. It lasted about an hour and a half. The next day I had the script conference with Larry Flynt, which lasted eight hours, because this film is about him, *his* life; yet this man had an unbelievably incredible attitude. He went through it meticulously, page by page, line by line, and he'd say [affecting an impersonation], "I wouldn't say that."

And I'd say, "Well, what would you say, Larry?"

And he'd say, "I'd say this, this, and this."

And I said, "Well Larry, what we have in the script is much more to the point."

And Larry would say, "Well listen, you are the director, that's your responsibility. I'm just telling you; you do what you want."

What was Larry Flynt's major concern about the script or about what the final product would be like?

There was not a major concern. There was just concern about what I'd call unimportant details, such as I mentioned. Larry understood that if he were to insist that the film be more favorable to him than he deserved, then I wouldn't make it.

He knew that?

I think he knew that. Because for me, either I'll make a film the way I see it, or I will not make it. So he understood immediately that there was no way to try to maneuver me somehow.

So he must have trusted you right from the beginning?

I guess. I didn't ask him, but I suspect he'd seen my other films and realized that I'm not a... you know.

What do you hope people will come away with thinking about a person like Larry Flynt?

I'm not trying to change anybody's life or anybody's mind. It was just fascinating for me, personally, from the start of hearing the name "Flynt" to the last day of shooting, how much more there is to a person than the labels we put on them, in both bad and good ways.

Do you think that the same holds true for people like Jerry Falwell and Charles Keating?

Oh yeah. Definitely. Definitely.

I'm sure people reading this book are going to find interesting the differences between what Scott and Larry originally wrote and the final results. A prime difference being how dialogue altered as the result of ad-libbing. Why do you do it, how does it work, and do you ever get scared that it might not work?

I believe ad-libbing is something that you must not rely on. First, you always have to start with a script that, if nothing unexpected happens, still stands solid so that you can make a good movie. But, as we talked about earlier, the better a script is, the more it opens itself to outside input. Then everything, of course, depends on the actors. Some actors really can't ad-lib. Some do, but it comes out too much like diarrhea. It's very rarely that you find an actor and actress, together, who not only get into their parts but let the characters overpower them. When that happens, and they start to ad-lib, sometimes they're not even aware of it. Then the ad-libbing comes from the characters and not the actors. When that happens, you'd be absolutely foolish not to use it, because those are the moments that bring more life, more spontaneity, and more credibility to the characters.

And for writers who have spent the last five years perfecting a line of dialogue into an exquisite jewel, what would you tell them?

You know, the problem is that very often writers really do spend hours figuring out the most perfect dialogue, but in life we don't have time to think about our lines. We react spontaneously. It's somehow boring when you are watching a movie and you sense that everybody is just repeating something, that it's not the characters talking to you, it's the author talking to you; and that all the lines prepared beforehand are now just being beautifully repeated. For me, it's somehow less interesting than when you have the feeling that what you are watching is just happening, right there in front of the camera, for the first time. That it's an unrepeatable moment. It's more exciting.

You see, a screenplay is not literature, and a writer's pride is his way with words, which is totally useless in a film script when it comes to description, though it is useful when it comes to dialogue; but even then the writer's personality has to step aside and let the characters' personalities talk.

Likewise, this must couple with your practice of casting people who most closely **are** *the characters, whether they're professional actors or not.*

You never find somebody, an actor, who is exactly the character you thought of, sitting at the table and writing. So it would be somehow silly, in my opinion, when you finally find an actress or an actor who is close to the character, to then not use their personality but, instead, try to cut them into the mold of what you were thinking they were when you were sitting at the table writing it.

I could imagine some actors might be intimidated to try ad-libbing. How do you know if they're capable or not?

I know beforehand. I know it from the screen test. Ad-libbing is a talent that an actor or actress either has or doesn't have. I choose a scene for the screen test—the scene is short—one page long. During the screen test, I encourage the actors. I say, "Start here, you know what the scene is about," and just let it go. Then I know if they are capable of doing it or not.

How did you cast the part of Larry Flynt?

Larry Flynt was one of the few characters I agreed would be mutually approved of by me and the studio. First, I got a list from the studio, of actors acceptable to them. And to be honest, before I met Woody Harrelson, I was very intrigued by their suggestion of Bill Murray. But it was surprising to me that he never, ever answered my calls. Then I met Woody Harrelson, and I was set from the moment I met the guy.

And when did the idea of casting Brett Harrelson as Larry Flynt's younger brother come in?

That was very funny. Once, Woody and I were sitting, talking, and he just mentioned, "Jesus Christ, my brother something this or that…"

And I sat up and said, "You have a brother?"

"Yeah."

"Older?"

"No, younger."

"My God!" I thought, "Can I meet him? Just for kicks." I got a kick out of the fact that brothers could be playing brothers. And Brett turned out, in my opinion, wonderfully.

How about Courtney Love, who is extremely talented but wouldn't normally be considered for the lead in a Hollywood studio film?

Well, Courtney, I didn't even know who she was, of course. She was brought in by our casting director, Francine Maisler who, by the way, is brilliant. Immediately, when Courtney came in, I was intrigued. I was not at all sure at the first moment whether she was Althea, but I knew that I was in the presence of a really extraordinary, special kind of personality.

In the film, we see Flynt's assailant, but he remains anonymous and silent. Do you have any idea who actually shot Larry Flynt?

Well, what I heard—but this is not confirmed, I'd have to check—is that finally the FBI (to get Larry's lawyers off its back) came across a prisoner who was imprisoned for I don't know how many consecutive life sentences as a hired murderer. He was supposed to have told his cellmate that he was the one who tried to shoot Larry Flynt. And from what I heard, nobody believed him. It's been speculated that the FBI just found somebody who would never get out of prison anyway and told him it might make his life a little easier if he confessed to this. But as I'm saying, it's just a rumor I heard. The fact is, no assailant was ever brought to justice. That's the fact.

You certainly had a challenge with this material—how to make a pornographer sympathetic.

Well, it's not at issue whether it is the pornography that will make the character sympathetic or not. I don't have any sympathy for pornography myself.

The challenge is to show the contradictions and the ambiguities of life. In this case, you can say that America rose to its best only by being provoked by its worst. This is one of the dilemmas we have to morally and philosophically deal with. In other words, if it weren't for "the worst" we wouldn't have the best.

For me, the most important line in the film is what Larry says at one trial: "America is the strongest country in the world because it is the freest country." That's what these pro-censorship moralists don't realize. They want to drag this country down. They don't understand that this country is not the strongest in the world because it's the *biggest*. China is bigger. Russia is bigger. It's not the strongest because it is the *richest* country in the world either. Other countries have far greater riches. No, this country is the strongest because it is the *freest*. And those who are crying out that we must take care of our so-called moral purity and morality are actually trying to drag the country down with their own quests for power.

Finally, then, what would you say to the person who asks, "Why should I pay to see a movie about Larry Flynt?"

I'm not trying to convince anybody to go and see my movies, *but* it's not only about Larry Flynt. It's about other people, too. And it's about issues other than pornography and censorship. All I tried to do was make the trip entertaining.

APPENDICES

THE LETTER AND TREATMENT SCOTT ALEXANDER & LARRY KARASZEWSKI SENT TO OLIVER STONE

November 11, 1993

To: Oliver Stone

Enclosed is our treatment for a darkly comic biopic of Larry Flynt. His life is the ultimate twisted American dream: Born in a log cabin, self-made millionaire, ran for President, gunned down... while never compromising his steadfastly-held principles. Larry has defined his life by testing the envelope of free speech. He sincerely believes that unless any man can say literally anything, this is not truly a free country.

We hope you enjoy it.

Scott Alexander **Larry Karaszewski**

PROLOGUE

In dirt-poor Appalachia, Larry's a little boy. His family are sharecroppers. Drunk Dad chases the kids with a shotgun. Larry never finishes grade school, but totally buys into the American dream: This is a great country, and anyone can be a success.

ACT ONE

1973. Larry's 30. In southern Ohio, he's a "huge success." He's opening his eighth *Hustler* go-go bar, but expanding too fast. Creditors come after him. But Larry's not dissuaded: This'll only make him stronger. He starts a newsletter to promote the nightclubs ("Fuzzy will be appearing Tuesday night.... Twinkle on Friday...")

Larry meets seventeen-year-old stripper Althea. She becomes the love of his life—he's never met anyone as deviant as himself. She's bisexual, occasionally trying out other women before handing them over to Larry.

Larry's newsletter becomes a glossy magazine and takes off. It's the first porno for "his people": the antithesis of the *Playboy* Man, with his penthouse, martini, and hi-fi stereo. *Hustler* is just crude blue-collar thinking. Society is shocked and outraged at its success. It's the most disgusting mainstream publication in history.

Money flows in. Larry buys an Ohio mansion. He puts a replica of his childhood log cabin in the basement.

A vengeful, highly offended Cincinnati sheriff goes after Larry and the magazine. He is charged with obscenity, as well as trumped-up counts of pandering and organized crime.

But Larry totally believes in the Bill of Rights, specifically the First Amendment. The mark of a great country is they leave you alone. Unless you can push a law to the absolute envelope, it's not worth anything.

So he brazenly takes the offensive—spending a fortune on principle. He sends 400,000 pamphlets to Ohio families: VIETNAM VIOLENCE IS THE REAL OBSCENITY. He buys full-page ads in national newspapers, with leading liberals, the ACLU, and free-speech advocates supporting his cause. Larry becomes a national issue.

However, Cincinnati throws the book at him—Larry is sentenced to seven to twenty-four years in prison. But he sees the bright side: Acquittals don't sell magazines...convictions do. It's insane free publicity. Every curious American buys the magazine. *Hustler* is unstoppable. It's soon raking in $20 million a year.

ACT TWO

Larry's conviction is overturned, and he gets released. The magazine begins hotheadedly going after political corruption. Deluded, Larry thinks he's earned his place alongside the free-speech intelligentsia who supported him during the trial...but no. He has no respectability. He thinks he's Thomas Paine, but the world thinks he's a gutter pornographer.

It's 1977. Carter's in office. Desperately seeking acceptance, Larry buys the Plains, Georgia, newspaper. Then he starts hanging out with the president's sister, evangelist Ruth Carter Stapleton. Finally, on a chartered plane, he unexpectedly gets born again.

The whole magazine changes. It becomes a berserk combination of sex and religion. There are still naked women, but now they're nailed on crucifixes. Jesus is on the masthead. Larry beams at perplexed Althea: "Now we're hustling for the Lord."

This mix of sex and religion pisses people off. Sales drop. But Larry doesn't care—he's famous. He can prove any point. Dozens of cities are chasing him down with obscenity charges, so he goes to Atlanta and brashly gets himself arrested. He will test the obscenity laws.

1978. While entering the Atlanta courthouse, he is shot.

Eight months in the hospital. Larry's in incredible pain. His intestine gets removed. Nobody is ever arrested in the shooting. Larry babbles endless conspiracy theories behind who gunned him down: JFK, FBI, KKK, Charles Keating, the Mob.... Finally he can't handle his day-to-day existence, and he puts Althea in charge of the corporation. Then Larry starts taking massive drugs for the pain, disappearing into a dark miserable haze....

1983. Larry emerges from the darkness... and five years have invisibly passed.

It's now a different era—Reagan's in office. Larry has surgery to sever the nerves to his legs. He'll never walk again, but the pain will be gone. He kicks the drugs and is now revitalized, but with a horribly changed vision of the country: America turned its back on him. He doesn't believe in the dream anymore.

Bitter, he sets out to create chaos. Larry takes on the world. He assembles a private Uzi-toting army. He magically connects himself to every ugly scandal of the day: the Vicki

Morgan murder; the naked congressman on Flight 007; John DeLorean's drug sting. He confronts every hypocrite in sight: a cartoon of Warren Burger being sodomized...a parody booze ad with Jerry Falwell screwing his mother.

Finally Larry produces the FBI tape of the DeLorean drug buy. He is dragged into court to reveal his source. He shows up wearing a diaper made of the American flag. The judge fines him for contempt of court. Larry arrogantly has *Hustler* Honies in hotpants pay the $10,000 fines in crumpled one-dollar bills.

Larry declares himself candidate for president. He promises to paint the White House pink. He names Indian activist Russell Means his vice president. He will make teachers the highest-paid employees. Larry is appealing to the underprivileged, the minorities, everybody who has been screwed by the system. "Every black will vote for me. Every Jew will vote for me. Every white cracker will vote for me. Every reader of *Hustler* will vote for me. I *am* the next president of the United States." Larry is terrifying the Washington establishment. He's throwing money everywhere, like Perot, to disrupt the status quo. He's a serious threat to the national order.

Althea begins using the drugs that Larry kicked. She becomes a full-blown junkie.

Larry's behavior is becoming dangerously irrational. In court again, he shouts obscenities and throws an orange at the judge. They order him to jail. He doesn't care: "I'm a rich white man, I'll just get some country club." *But no.* The Feds are out to shut him up. He is carted off to a hellhole psychiatric prison.

ACT THREE

Inside, they break him. Rumors abound Larry's been lobotomized. Nobody knows for sure what happened, but he is now totally mad. He abruptly withdraws the candidacy. And Althea contracts AIDS.

Meanwhile, Jerry Falwell has seen the *Hustler* ad parody. In the manner of a Dewar's Profile, it tastelessly depicts Falwell stating he screwed his mother in an outhouse.

Falwell is insanely offended. Upset, he sues Larry for slander. Then Falwell xeroxes the ad and sends a million copies to "his people," to raise money for a legal fight.

Defiant, Larry countersues for copyright infringement.

The case goes to federal district court. Larry is yanked from prison to testify. His lawyers calmly advise: It's an easy case to win—the ad clearly stated "just a parody." But Larry gets on the stand, sees the hated hypocrite Falwell...and goes wacko. He crazily admits he has a personal vendetta and wanted to "assassinate" Falwell's integrity. Larry bizarrely claims he has, locked in a safe, three signed affidavits stating that Falwell *did* screw his mother. The court becomes a shambles. Falwell wins for emotional distress.

Althea finally dies of AIDS. Falwell is on TV, stating it's a disease sent from God. Larry sets out to kick Falwell's ass.

Larry appeals all the way to the United States Supreme Court. In a landmark decision, they reverse the lower courts and actually side with *Hustler.* It's an incredible free-speech victory. In the proudest moment of Larry Flynt's life, he has beaten the Moral Majority while winning a place in the history books. The system agrees with him. He can believe in America again.

CAST AND CREW CREDITS

COLUMBIA PICTURES presents
In Association with Phoenix Pictures
An Ixtlan Production

Woody Harrelson   Courtney Love   Edward Norton

In A Milos Forman Film

"THE PEOPLE VS. LARRY FLYNT"

James Cromwell	Brett Harrelson	Vincent Schiavelli	D'Army Bailey
Crispin Glover	Donna Hanover	Miles Chapin	Burt Neuborne
James Carville	Norm McDonald	Richard Paul	Jan Triska

Casting by
Francine Maisler, C.S.A.

Film Editor
Christopher Tellefsen

Produced by
Oliver Stone
Janet Yang and
Michael Hausman

Music by
Thomas Newman

Production Designer
Patrizia Von Brandenstein

Directed by
Milos Forman

Costume Designers
Theodor Pistek
Arianne Phillips

Director of Photography
Philippe Rousselot, A.F.C.

Written by
Scott Alexander
& Larry Karaszewski

Cast

Larry Flynt . . . . Woody Harrelson
Althea Leasure . . . . Courtney Love
Isaacman . . . . Edward Norton
Jimmy Flynt . . . . Brett Harrelson
Ruth Carter Stapleton . . . . Donna Hanover
Charles Keating . . . . James Cromwell
Arlo . . . . Crispin Glover
Chester . . . . Vincent Schiavelli
Miles . . . . Miles Chapin
Simon Leis . . . . James Carville
Jerry Falwell . . . . Richard Paul
Roy Grutman . . . . Burt Neuborne
The Assassin . . . . Jan Triska
10 Year Old Larry . . . . Cody Block
8 Year Old Jimmy . . . . Ryan Post
Old Hillbilly . . . . Robert Davis
Young Ma Flynt . . . . Kacky Walton
Young Pa Flynt . . . . John Ryan
1st Stripper . . . . Kathleen Kane

Disc Jockey . . . . Greg Roberson
Old Printer . . . . Jim Peck
Trucker . . . . Mike Pniewski
Staffers . . . . Tim Parati
                                          Rick Rogers
                                          Dan Lenzini
                                          David Compton
                                          Gary Lowery
Stills Photographer . . . . Stephen Dupree
Tovah . . . . Rainbeau Mars
News Dealer . . . . Tam Drummond
Ma Flynt . . . . Nancy Lea Owen
Pa Flynt . . . . John Fergus Ryan
Governor Rhodes . . . . Oliver Reed
Jacuzzi Girls . . . . Meresa T. Ferguson
                                          Andrena Fisher
Police Detective . . . . Ken Kidd
Judge Morrissey (Cincinatti Court) . . Larry Flynt
Jury Forewoman (Cincinatti Court) . . . Janie Paris

Court Clerk (Cincinatti Court)
.... Carol Russell-Woloshin
Rally Singer .... Ruby Wilson
Announcer at Rally .... Eddie Davis
Ad Sales Guy .... Blaine Pickett
European Photographer .... Ladi von Jansky
Georgia Cops .... Kerry White
Joey Hadley
Robert Stapleton .... Chris Schadrack
Georgia Prosecuter .... Mac Pirkle
Georgia Doctor .... Mark W. Johnson
Flynt's Personal Bodyguard .... Doug Bauer
Bodyguard .... Roberto Roman Ramirez
Dr. Bob .... Blaine Nashold, M.D.
Cute Receptionist .... Aurelia Thierree
Blow Dried Jerk .... Scott Winters
Judge Thomas Mantke (LA Court) D'Army Bailey
Lawyer (LA Court) .... Mike McLaren
CBS Lawyer .... Andrew Stahl
Delorean Attorney .... Michael Detroit
Keating's Secretary .... Jaime Jackson
Federal Marshall .... David Dwyer
Deputy Marshalls .... Richard Birdsong
James A. White
Butler .... Gerry Robert Byrne
Bailiff (LA Court) .... Benjamin Greene, Jr.
Mantke Clerk .... Mary Neal Naylor
Springfield Prison Guard .... Tina M. Bates
Divinity Students .... Evans Donnell
Jay Adams

Dean of Liberty College .... Bennett Wood
Judge Kirk (Roanoke Court) ..... Janice Holder
Jury Foreman (Roanoke Court) . A.V. McDowell
Chief Justice Rhenquist .... Jim Grimshaw
Justice Marshall .... James Smith
Justice Scalia .... Rand Hopkins
Justice Stevens .... Charles M. Crump
Supreme Court Marshall .... Pierre Secher
Svelte Reporter .... Linn Sitler
Reporters .... Mary M. Norman
Jack Shea
Lisa Lax
Georgia Reporters .... Susan Howe
Michael Davis
Dennis Turner
Patti Hatchett
Ann Marie Hall
Nate Bynum
Paula Haddock
Gary Kraen
Slick Reporter .... Norm McDonald
L.A. Reporter .... Jeff Johnson
Falwell Reporters .... Joey Sulipeck
Jim Palmer
DC Reporters .... Gene Lyons
Saida Pagan
James Hild
Michael Klastorin
TV Reporter at Supreme Court
.... Michelle Robinson

Crew

Associate Producers .... Scott Ferguson
George Linardos
Unit Production Manager .... Michael Hausman
1st Assistant Director .... David McGiffert
2nd Assistant Director .... Scott Harris
Production Supervisor .... Gerry Robert Byrne
Art Director .... James Nezda
Shawn Hausman
Set Decorators .... Maria A. Nay
Amy Wells
Assistant Art Directors ... James Flood Truesdale
James Feng
Script Supervisor .... Ann Gyory
A Camera Operator .... Anastas N. Michos
B Camera Operator .... Ted Morris
First Assistant Camera .... Robin Melhuish
Brian Nordheim

Costume Supervisor .... Nancy McArdle
Costumers .... Lawrence Velasco
Stephanie Colin
Key Makeup .... Ben Nye
Bron Roylance
Hairstylist .... Melissa A. Yonkey
Chief Lighting Technician .... Jack English
Best Boy .... James Babineaux
Rigging Gaffer .... Robert D. Carrier
Key Grip .... J. Wayne Parker
Dolly Grip .... Chris Rawlins, Jr.
Key Rigging Grips .... Riko Schatke
Henry M. Massey
Stunt Coordinator .... Tim Trella
Special Effects .... Rodman Kiser
Production Coordinator .... Chrissie Davis

Assistant Production Coordinators
. . . . Kimberly N. Fajen
Margo Hunt
Jennifer Silverman
Jennifer Jenkins
Production Accountant . . . . Matilde P. Valera
Assistant to Mr. Harrelson . . . . . . Danielle Tahos
Assistant to Ms. Love . . . . . Raphael T.S. Murray
Assistant to Mr. Forman . . . . . Martina Zborilova
Assistant to Mr. Stone . . . . Annie Mei-Ling Tien
Assistant to Ms. Yang . . . . Janet Monaghan
Location Manager . . . . Betsy Bottando
Assistant Location Manager . . . . . . Diana Strauss
Property Master . . . . Bill Dambra
Assistant Property Master . . . . . David Chamerski
Buyer . . . . Sarah Young
Construction Coordinator . . . . Tyler Osman
Construction Shop Manager . Henning Molfenter
Construction Foreman . . . . Troy Osman
Scenic Artist . . . . John Snow
Camera Scenic Artist . . . . Lee Ross
Lead Person . . . . Leonard Spears
Key Set Dresser . . . . David Weathers
On Set Dresser . . . . Spencer Register
Transportation Captain . . . . Jerry Jackson
Transportation Co-Captain . . . . Rick Davis
Sound Mixer . . . . Chris Newman
Boom Operator . . . . Marc-Jon Sullivan
Cable Person . . . . Gregg Harris
First Assistant Editor . . . . Joel Hirsch
Assistant Editor . . . . Misako Shimizu
Supervising Sound Editor . . . . Stan Bochner
Music Editor . . . . Bill Bernstein
Sound FX Editors . . . . .P. DeMetrius
Richard Quentin King
ADR Editor . . . . Hal Levinsohn
Foley Editor . . . . Ira Spiegel
Foley Mixer . . . . George Lara

Re-Recording Mixer . . . . Michael Barry
Music Recorded at . . . . Village Recorder
Todd A/O
Video Assist . . . . Frankie Yario, Jr.
Second Second Assistant Director Stephen Hagen
Production Assistants . . . . John R. Saunders
Tobia Minckler
Doug Campbell
Darian Corby
John Brudenell
Barry Barclay
Heather Ross
Steven Samanen
Jana Triska
Karym Usher
Draper . . . . Shari Griffin
Publicist . . . . Michael Klastorin
Still Photographer . . . . Sidney Baldwin
Casting Associates . . . . Kathryn Eisenstein
Kathleen Driscoll-Mohler
Extras Casting . . . . Willo Hausman
Kate Kennedy
Mid South Casting . . . . Jo Doster
Kim Petrosky
Researchers   Ashley Cook
Barry Gildea
Mr. Harrelson's Dialect Coach . . . Nadia Venesse
Security for Mr. Harrelson . . . . Steve Ranger
Catering . . . . Unique Catering
Craft Service . . . . Wende L. Martin
First Aid . . . . Safety Emergency Services
Process Projection by . . . The Bran Ferren Group
Color Timer . . . . David Pultz
Negative Cutter . . . . J.G. Films
Main and End Titles by Balsmeyer & Everett, Inc.
Opticals by . . . . The Effects House
Color by . . . . DuArt

Consultant
Alan L. Isaacman
Isaacman, Kaufman & Painter

Soundtrack On Angel / EMI Records

Columbia Pictures is the author of this film (motion picture)
for the purpose of copyright and other laws.

Special Thanks to

The Supreme Court of the United States

Dr. W.W. Herenton, Mayor of Memphis

Jim Rout, Mayor of Shelby County

The Memphis & Shelby Co. Film,
Tape and Music Commission

Tennessee Film, Entertainment
& Music Commission

Shel Bachrach

Filmed in PANAVISION®
Prints by TECHNICOLOR®
DOLBY
SDDS

This picture is based upon actual events. However, some of the characters, incidents portrayed and names used are fictitious, and any similarity of such to the name, character, or history of any actual person is entirely coincidental and unintentional.

The animals used in this film were in no way mistreated and all scenes in which they appeared were under strict supervision with the utmost concern for their handling.

This motion picture photoplay is protected pursuant to the provisions of the laws of the United States of America and other countries. Any unauthorized duplication and/or distribution of this photoplay may result in civil liability and criminal prosecution

A COLUMBIA PICTURES RELEASE
A SONY PICTURES ENTERTAINMENT COMPANY

Credits not final at the time of publication.

ABOUT THE AUTHORS

Scott Alexander & Larry Karaszewski first met as roommates in their freshman year at the University of Southern California. On a whim, they decided to write a screenplay during their senior year, which sold a week after they graduated from USC's School of Cinema. Their first produced film was the highly successful *Problem Child,* which they followed with *Problem Child 2;* they were later spun off into a cartoon series and a movie for television.

They then changed direction and wrote the highly acclaimed "biopic" script, *Ed Wood,* which was directed by Tim Burton and won for them a Writer's Guild nomination for Best Screenplay of the Year. They followed this with another biopic, *The People vs. Larry Flynt,* which was chosen to be the closing film in the New York Film Festival. During this time, they also completed screenplays for the Disney remake of *That Darn Cat* and the science fiction extravaganza, *Mars Attacks,* which reunited them with Tim Burton.

Alexander, a native of Los Angeles, started his Hollywood career toiling on low-budget horror films as a music editor. As a director, his work has appeared on MTV and Nickelodeon, and his short films have won numerous awards. He has written for HBO's *Tales from the Crypt* and the television series *Monsters,* which he also directed. He lives in Los Angeles with his wife, Debbie, and two sons, Casey and Jeremy.

Karaszewski, who was born and raised in South Bend, Indiana, worked as a film critic for an NBC affiliate's nightly news program before writing and directing *Beyond Our Control,* a weekly half-hour satirical television show. The Midwest-based series won the Grand Prize Award for television at the Chicago International Film Festival. He lives in Hollywood with his wife, Emily, and two children, Carver and Jack.

Adam Davidson, a writer and director, won the 1991 Academy Award for Best Live Action Short, *The Lunch Date.* He and Milos Forman collaborated and became friends while working on the ill-fated *Hell Camp.* He conducted his interviews with Forman exclusively for the afterword of this book in September 1996. He lives in Santa Monica, California.